Supervillain of the Day

SUPERVILLAIN OF THE DAY

SUPERVILLAIN HUNTERS, INTERNATIONAL

by Katie Lynn Daniels

Cover design by Jordan Miller
Interior formatting by Aubrey Hansen

Special thanks to Elizabeth Kirkwood for reading absolutely everything I sent her, however meaningless; to Jordan Miller for his brilliant cover designs; to Elsa for her meticulous editing an invaluable assistance in revising; to Aubrey Hansen for helping clueless me with formatting and never getting tired of reading these books.

Published by:
Provide Your Own – Books
PO Box 748
Tompkinsville, KY 42167
Website: Books.ProvideYourOwn.com

Print Edition, June 2013
ISBN-13: 978-0615815015 (Provide Your Own - Books)
ISBN-10: 0615815014
Library of Congress Control Number: 2013910170

This is a work of fiction. Any similarities to real people, living or dead, are merely coincidental.

For Boots
For every dance
And every smile
And every laugh

TABLE OF CONTENTS

AUTHOR'S NOTE

The stories so far have all been set in London and the surrounding countryside. This raises the obvious question of what is going on in the rest of the world? Has everyone died from neglect? Has civilization been overrun by villainy? Is the author simply ignoring their existence for the sake of Plot?

In the first book, recall, there were Supervillains everywhere but London. Has the situation reversed itself and all masters of villainy focused their efforts on Floyd's stronghold?

The answer to such questions is this—the rest of the world is alive and well, and the supervillains are wreaking their own peculiar sort of havoc all over. Each nation is dealing with it in their own way. Romania has a supervillain dictator, Russia has moved entirely underground, and the United States...

Well, you know what those Americans are like, with their cars and their comic books and their extraordinary right to bear arms. Villainy has their hands full with that lot, I'm telling you.

But that's what this story is about...

A TYPICAL NIGHT

Night is the period during a 24 hour day in which there is no sunlight. Other indications that it is night are the presence of stars or moonlight. Night is usually cooler than day. Poetic phrases associated with night include words like calm, peaceful, beautiful, quiet, and ethereal. Lullabies are written to be sung at night to help one go to sleep. Sleep is usually partaken in at night. Night is considered romantic and beautiful.

The only resemblance the night in question had to any of the above is that it was more or less dark, and there was no sunlight. The sound of traffic on the A730 shattered any illusion of quiet or silence. From nearby lighted windows came the sound of talking and music and laughter. Rats of both the human and the rodent variety scurried about getting into trash and causing havoc. And on a broad street with little nocturnal traffic, two men were having it out in a street brawl.

One was a laughing, taunting, two-faced villain, literally. His head had two faces, and he could swivel completely to show one or the other.

1

One face was laughing cruelly, and the other was angry and hateful, and he switched between them at will, attempting to catch his opponent off guard.

His opponent was small and lithe and clearly knew what he was doing. His face was set in hard, straight lines, impervious to the villain's attempts to distract him, but he was losing all the same. Two-Face had the advantage of height and weight and of having nowhere else he wanted to be. His opponent had had a very long day, was very tired of trying to outwit supervillains, and just wanted to go home and sleep.

His name was Jeffry Lewis Floyd, he was a reporter, and he had just had a very trying argument with the editor the paper he worked for about whether or not supervillain stories were out of style. The Editor had said they were. Floyd had insisted they weren't. Floyd had lost the argument to the infallible declaration that the editor knows what is best for his paper, based on the fact that the editor is the one who signs the checks, and he really didn't want to be fighting at this moment.

Two-Face didn't give him a choice. He was an irritating nuisance, but certainly not one Floyd considered worth losing a good night's sleep over, and that was why he was losing this particular fight.

Floyd was looking around desperately for some way to duck out of the fight, give Two-Face the slip and go home, but no opportunities presented itself, and the attempt only distracted him further. He was standing on a sidewalk, next to a four lane street. The sidewalk was paved and modern, with trees planted in little square holes at precise distances. The other side of the sidewalk was lined with buildings. All sorts of buildings. Offices, restaurants, and department stores all squeezed in next to each other and polished to a proper modern shine.

Floyd's thoughts were interrupted when Two-Face hit him. He fell to the ground, rolled, stood up, touched his jaw gingerly, and glowered at his opponent. The fight degenerated into Floyd trying his best not to be hit while putting very little effort into fighting back. Finally Two-Face had enough fun, and decided to end things.

Stepping back for a moment he put his fingers in his mouth and whistled. This jerked Floyd's wandering thoughts back to the real world, and he looked around for whatever new danger was about to present itself. He also looked for somewhere to run, but all he saw were the same things that had been there before: wide, open pavement lined with empty, dark, locked buildings.

He suddenly had the uneasy feeling that someone was sneering at him and looked back at Two-Face. Behind the villain loomed a larger figure. This one had a look of pure evil joy on his face, and he stood a full head taller than Two-Face, which gave him at least eighteen inches on Floyd. Floyd sighed deeply and pondered the end of his supervillain fighting career.

Two-Face introduced his new friend as Brawn. He chuckled, then laughed, then threw his head back and crowed in amusement, before finally composing himself and explaining to Floyd what his new friend was going to do to him. Brawn's face twisted in what might have passed for a smile if it had been less hideous.

For the time being, Two-Face was content to step aside and let his new partner finish his job. Motivated out of a sense of self-preservation, Floyd dodged the two huge fists that were swung at him, dropped, rolled, and came up behind the brute, but he forgot that that's exactly where Two-Face was standing, waiting to knock him down again. This time, before he could recover and regain his feet, the brute picked him up and, in a fit of rage, threw him against the nearest building.

The glass show window shattered under the force of having a body hurled into it, and Floyd went flying backward, knocking over several mannequins on the way, into the heart of a lady's dress store.

He didn't get back up.

Outside, Two-Face and Brawn waited eagerly for their opponent to reappear, and were puzzled when he didn't. Their puzzlement was cut short by the sound of approaching police sirens responding to what was reported on their computers as a break-in.

It was at this point that most crooks would have cut their losses and left. Better not to get caught in front of a department store with a smashed window. But Two-Face and his oversized buddy weren't most crooks, they were supervillains—few of which are known for doing the smart thing at any given point. They stayed.

"Police! Put your hands up!"

Grinning, Two-Face obeyed. "We don't want no trouble, officer," he drawled. "We didn't do nothin', promise. We were just standing here when that man busted the window."

Brawn nodded enthusiastic agreement.

"What man?" the officer asked briskly.

4

Two-Face shrugged, keeping his hands in the air. "Short," he said. "Dark hair. Mean look about him."

"Which way did he go?"

Two-Face inclined his head towards the broken window. "Inside," he said.

"Wait here," the officer ordered. "We'll want to get your statement later."

He and the other police headed towards the department store. Two-Face and Brawn waited until they were all past, and then attacked from the rear.

When Floyd heard the sirens, he didn't get up. It was when no one put him in handcuffs and told him to come along nicely that he got curious and looked to see what was going on.

Several more police cars were arriving, and Two-Face and Brawn were beginning to lose the upper hand. Two-Face had even begun to lose the self-satisfied smirk on one of his faces, and he raised his fingers to his mouth and whistled again. Two short, ear-piercing blasts.

Two minutes later the street was crawling with more villains, surrounding the policemen who surrounded Two-Face and Brawn. Floyd stood in the department store window and watched them, momentarily battling with his conscience. He should be out there, helping in the fight of law and order against evil and chaos. That was the right thing to do.

Right thing or not, Floyd still wanted nothing more then to go home and sleep, so he shrugged, and settled on watching the battle instead.

More police arrived. Floyd began to consider possible back door exits, but the battle had finally

5

begun to interest him. It was beginning to turn into a small war.

Surprisingly, it was the supervillains who lost interest. The sky had begun to lighten imperceptibly, and Two-Face finally decided that the best thing to do was the vacate the premises, and his buddies followed him. He paused after assaulting a police officer, however, looked straight at Floyd, and showed his evilest grinning face.

Floyd shivered. The villain had known he'd been standing there the whole time, and he didn't like that. He didn't like it at all. Now he wished he'd gone out and joined the fray, but if there was one thing he'd learned it was that you couldn't go back in time. He stepped cautiously out of the display window, unable to shake the vague, uneasy feeling that the grin had left imprinted on his brain.

He didn't hear the sound of every police officer suddenly pointing a taser at him, but he sensed it and he stopped instinctively. He glanced around, saw the looks of hostility, and raised both hands above his head.

Slowly. *Very* slowly. It had already been a long night, and he really didn't want anything else to go wrong.

Floyd didn't say anything. The policemen didn't stay anything. Floyd kept his hands up and waited. No one continued to say anything.

"I didn't intentionally break the window," Floyd said finally, licking his lips nervously. "I was thrown there."

Silence.

"By Two-Face's nasty friend," he added unhelpfully.

There was a rustle at the back of the crowd.

"Hey, it's okay!" a familiar voice shouted. "I know this guy. He's all right."

The policemen visibly relaxed. The officer who was talking stepped into view.

"Joseph," Floyd said in relief. "I'm very glad to see you."

"Go home," Adams told him, without returning his greeting. "Everything's under control here."

His brusque attitude surprised Floyd, but he was too tired to protest. He went home.

....

Floyd hated mornings, especially when they were in the middle of the day. Especially when he'd overslept. Despite the fact that he'd accustomed himself to Earth's 24 hour daylight period, he couldn't shake the feeling that a proper night's sleep was six hours, and anything longer than that left him disoriented and moody.

He was usually awake and at work by the time the sun came up in the morning, but by the time he sat up and wondered at what point in the previous day he'd been run over by a bulldozer, it was after noon. That thought was so startling that it scared all the other thoughts out of his brain. It seemed particularly significant for some reason, but he couldn't remember any appointments he'd had.

It was a feeling that bothered him. He was also bothered by something else, something in connection with why he felt like he'd been run over by a bulldozer, but he told that something to shut up and go away until he figured out why he felt like there was somewhere he was supposed to be at noon on Thursday.

Thursday! He checked his watch and verified. It was indeed Thursday, and it was 12:55 local time. Grumbling in a language that wasn't English, and wasn't very polite either, he forced himself out of bed, into clean clothes and into the brilliantly lit outside world, not even bothering to try and force his door to close all the way. Outside traffic rumbled, horns honked, people talked, the wind was blowing, and it was quite clearly the middle of the day. Floyd took one look at it and ran.

He ran past shoppers and students and business folk. He knocked down a small child, darted back to apologize, and then continued on his way. He elicited strange looks and the occasional insult, but he went too fast to hear them, and in ten minutes he was in a decidedly better mood. He almost ran past his destination, stopped abruptly, and heard the satisfying tinkle of a shop bell as he entered. He plopped into his usual seat, looked at Adams, and blinked.

Something was off.

"Good morning, officer," he said with genuine cheerfulness.

Adams didn't stir.

"I hope I haven't kept you waiting too long," Floyd pressed on, keeping his conscious mind occupied while his subconscious worked out what wasn't right. "I got detained last night, and overslept this morning and, you know how it goes. Alien planet and all."

He grinned at Adams, and waved the waitress over to give her his drink order. The only part of Adams that moved was his eyes, as he glanced first at Floyd, then at the waitress, and then back out the window to the busy street.

Floyd frowned.

"Is something wrong?" he asked abruptly.

Adams started, as though coming back to the real world. "No," he said abruptly. "Everything's fine."

"Oh." Floyd relaxed. His subconscious registered that as the first lie the police officer had ever told him, and kept on trying to figure things out.

"Thanks for getting me out of that jam last night," he continued. "I wasn't looking forward to the alternative."

Adams nodded absently, drifting back to wherever he'd been before Floyd had showed up.

Floyd frowned in concern. He drew his knees up to his chin, accepted the drink the waitress brought him, waved her off when she asked after their orders, and regarded Adams thoughtfully.

Something was definitely wrong.

"You're quiet today," he said finally. Adams didn't reply.

Floyd tried again.

"Am I in trouble?"

"No," Adams said shortly.

Floyd took over from his subconscious and began to analyze the situation. There were a lot of things bothering him today. He had almost forgotten to be here, he felt like he'd been run over by a bulldozer, and he hadn't properly sat down and remembered what had happened the previous day. He decided to start with that.

He'd been walking home from the offices of the London Star after a long argument with the Editor about the superhero trend. It was almost midnight. He'd been accosted by Two-Face. They'd fought. Or rather, Two-Face had fought and Floyd had tried to get away, and then Brawn had come along and thrown him through a department store window.

Well, that cleared up one thing, Floyd thought ruefully. A department store window would feel very similar to a bulldozer if one hit it the right way.

Then the police and the local villain conglomerate had had a showdown while he watched. He felt a twinge of guilt about the watching part, but decided to ignore it for the time being. He'd been held up by the police, and then Adams had come along and...

Floyd blinked.

"Something happened last night," he said abruptly.

"Nothing happened last night," Adams said too quickly.

"Yes, it did," Floyd argued. "You saved my hide and then you sent me home. You never get me out of a scrape and send me home. You always keep me around to lecture and help clean up and so forth. And when I came in today, you didn't say anything about me being late. You didn't say anything about last night. You didn't say anything at all. You've said two words since I walked in the door, and one was an outright lie. You never lie. Especially to me, because you're trying to be a good influence. So 'fess up and tell me; *what is wrong*?"

Adams smiled in spite of himself, but it was a sad, pathetic smile. He shifted in his seat and met Floyd's eyes briefly.

"I was suspended," he said simply.

If Floyd had been holding onto anything he would have dropped it, if he had been standing he would have sat, but since he was doing neither he simply stared in absolute disbelief.

"No," he said with conviction. "You suspended? Never."

Adams stopped looking at him.

"There must be some mistake," Floyd said firmly.

Adams shook his head.

"What happened?" Floyd demanded.

Adams shrugged. "I failed to fulfill my duty," he said, staring vacantly at the street.

"You were there," Floyd said pointedly. "You fought with the rest of them, which is more than I did. I stood in the display window and watched."

That was the first time Floyd realized that whatever had happened had been entirely his fault, and he promised himself that he would never again stand by and watch a fight without participating. Even a good night's sleep wasn't worth this haunting feeling of guilt.

"I'm sorry," he said abruptly.

Adams smiled wanly. "It's not your fault," he said gently.

"How do I know it's not my fault?" Floyd said hotly. "You haven't told me what happened yet."

"There were some papers I was supposed to be transporting safely," Adams said. "I lost them."

"Last night?"

"Yes."

"In the fight?"

"Yes."

"How is that your fault?"

Adams raised his eyebrows. "I was supposed to be transporting them safely," he repeated.

"There was a fight," Floyd said blankly.

"I should have stayed out of it."

"Joseph…"

"It's all right, Floyd, okay? It's my life."

Floyd shrugged. "Can you find the papers?"

"They were stolen."

"By who?"

"I didn't get a good look at him. Long black coat. Evil scowl."

Floyd cursed. "Two-Face," he said. "I hate that guy. Look, Joseph, that whole fight was my fault. You should just tell them that. They shouldn't blame you for it."

"Floyd," Adams said, shaking his head. "It was my job to make sure that accidents didn't befall the papers. I failed to protect them, from the fight, from the thief; from you, if you insist. It doesn't matter who took them. I should have prevented it."

"But they were supervillains!" Floyd exclaimed. "What were you supposed to do? Die?"

"I can't blame the supervillains," Adams said patiently. "You're the one who made sure of that."

"Huh?"

"You're the one who drew up those policies and convinced Inspector McCormick to present them to the police commissioner," Adams explained. "You're the one who said we should do our jobs regardless of supervillain activity."

Floyd shut his mouth.

"It's a good policy," Adams added hastily. "You were right about the force getting slack on things. I'm just pointing out that villains are no excuse for what happened."

"I'll get them back," Floyd swore. "Two-Face and I have a score to settle."

"Just let it go, Floyd."

"No!" he exclaimed. "This is my fault, all of it. The fight was started because of me, I didn't step in and try to help end it, I'm the one who suggested those policies..."

"Floyd," Adams said firmly.

Floyd looked crestfallen. "I'm sorry," he said contritely.

"It's all right," Adams said consolingly.

"No, it's not all right!" Floyd shouted. "Hang it, Joseph, I want to help!"

"There's nothing you can do."

"You watch me," Floyd said darkly. "If I can take out a dozen supervillains with my bare hands, then I can manage to find a few missing papers."

"Stay out of my business," Adams said crossly. "I didn't ask for your help."

"You don't have to ask for it," Floyd insisted. "That's what friends are for."

The words were out before he had a chance to bite them back and he matched glares with Adams as though he'd fully intended to say them.

"We're not friends," Adams said, standing. "We work together out of necessity and that's all. Understand?"

He didn't wait for an answer before leaving. Long before reaching the door, his anger dissipated into dejection, and the bell tinkling behind him sounded like a funeral dole.

AN UNTYPICAL DAY

Floyd had never been in the restaurant by himself before. Every Thursday, Adams was waiting for him when he arrived, no matter how late it was, and when Floyd left Adams stayed put as though he had all the time in the world. Having the police officer walk out on him was one of the most disconcerting things he'd experienced since meeting him. For several minutes, he simply stared at the empty chair across from him as though unable to quite comprehend it.

Unable to think of anything else to do he was about to follow Adams when he realized that being the last one at the table gave him the responsibility of paying for their drinks, something he'd never done before. By the time he finally returned to the wide open outdoors he'd decided that his day couldn't possibly get any weirder, and set about fixing it.

He decided to find Two-Face.

....

Deciding to find Two-Face and actually locating the villain were completely different prospects. During the past week, Floyd had seemed to encounter the villain every time he turned around, but now he seemed to have vanished into thin air without a trace of his existence left behind. Even Brawn couldn't be located, and it was usually hard to hide a brute like that.

He checked all the usual supervillain haunts. Nothing. He checked all the usual villain haunts. No one was talking. He tried lurking around in plain sight. No one turned up. He tried skulking around in dark alleyways and the worst parts of town. Still no one. Everyone was quiet and behaving and out of sight, and he didn't like it one bit. The reckless way he'd been behaving, he should have had at least two or three henchmen try to have it out with him, and at least one supervillain usually went at him each day.

It dawned on him, sitting on top of the roof of a tenement building, that it didn't matter who he was chasing after, he wouldn't have caught them that day. And he didn't like it. He didn't know what to do about it, and he didn't like that either.

Finally, he climbed down from his perch and betook himself to Scotland Yard. The clerk on duty looked up at him, brushing fine golden hair out of her eyes as she did so.

"Can I help?" she asked, and Floyd found himself suddenly tongue-tied and wondering what on earth he was doing there. He usually came to talk to Adams, and Adams wasn't here. He was at home. On suspension. And it was his fault.

The clerk was staring at him, waiting, blinking her long eyelashes patiently.

"Um," Floyd said. "I was just wondering. I've been out all day tracking down supervillains, and I haven't found one. Not even a henchman. And I thought that was very strange."

"They have their off days," she said. Her voice was musical, enchantingly beautiful, and extremely distracting. She didn't look like she belonged in a police station, she looked like she belonged in a beauty parlor.

"Do you have a name?" he asked abruptly. "And are you busy tonight?"

She laughed at him, but for some reason he didn't mind.

"Carly," she said, "And I just got on duty, so I'll be here until midnight."

"Well, in that case," he grinned.

"Why are you looking for supervillains?" she asked curiously. "Isn't that dangerous?"

"I'm a reporter," Floyd said. "Danger is my middle name."

She laughed again.

"Listen," Floyd said seriously. "The supervillain thing is bothering me, but there's something else bothering me too. I wonder if you could help me."

"If it involves going to get a drink," she said coyly, "I'm told you I'm on duty."

Floyd shook his head. "A friend of mine is in trouble," he said.

"Do you want to file an official report?" she asked, her manner all businesslike.

"No," Floyd shook his head. "My friend is a police officer."

"Does he have a name?"

"Sergeant Joseph S. Adams."

Her fingers flew across the keyboard. Her perfect forehead wrinkled in a frown.

"He's on suspension," she said, "pending a hearing on Monday."

"I know that," Floyd said. "That's why he's in trouble."

"I don't know what you expect me to do, Mr...."

"Floyd," Floyd said. "And drop the Mr. bit."

"What do you expect me to do?"

Floyd sighed. "I don't know," he admitted, running his fingers through his hair. "I was kind of hoping I could talk to his supervisor."

"Why would that do you any good?"

Because it's my fault, Floyd didn't say.

"I don't know," he repeated instead. "That's why I asked for your help."

"You don't even know me," she protested gently.

He smiled helplessly. "I know," he said. "But you looked nice."

She sighed and lowered her gaze back to the computer. "Chief Inspector Connery O'Rourke was the officer responsible for your friend's suspension," she said. "He's not here today."

"Do you know when he's coming in?"

"Tomorrow."

"When tomorrow?"

"His schedule says nine o' clock."

"Thank you," Floyd said, flashing another grin. "You've been most helpful. And I owe you a drink sometime."

He waltzed out of the station before she could reply, pretending to be happier and more carefree than he actually felt. He pondered going to renew his argument with his employer, but decided he was too depressed for that. He felt guilty going out and partying without having done anything to help Adams, so he went home, sat alone in the dark for a while, and finally went to sleep.

………

Friday morning started at 4 AM, a good hour before the sun came up, but Floyd still had an uneasy feeling of something bothering him. He remembered over email. Adams was in trouble and it was his fault. Grimly, Floyd decided that he hated feeling perpetually guilty, but this realization didn't help him come up with a better plan.

He ate something that passed for breakfast in his dictionary and went out early to see if he could catch some henchmen getting into trouble. London was surprisingly quiet and well behaved. There were no tipped-over trash cans, no broken windows, no piled up traffic as a result of a blocked road that should have been perfectly clear. The papers reported no force fields, UFOs, murders or conspiracy theories. The world looked almost normal.

Floyd didn't like it.

When the sun came up, Floyd didn't like that either. He went back to the police station.

There was a different clerk on duty, of course. An older lady with straight black hair and hawk-like eyes, that told the world she was tired of being at work, and waiting for her relief to come in at any minute.

"Can I help you?" she asked in a clipped, formal tone of voice.

"Yes," Floyd said with confidence he didn't feel. "Have there been any crimes reported today?"

The clerk lost her composure and blinked once or twice. "Excuse me?" she said. Her voice rose on the last syllable, coming out almost like a squawk.

"Have there been any crimes reported today?" Floyd repeated, carefully enunciating each word.

"I don't know what you mean," she said, unsure how to react.

"It's very simple," Floyd said patiently. "You've been here since midnight. The answer is either yes or no. Have there been any crimes reported today?"

She stared.

"Any at all?" he elaborated. "Anything? A single disturbance? A robbery? A false alarm? Anything?"

"No," she said finally. "The phone hasn't rung all night. Not that it's any of your business," she added in a clipped tone, finally regaining her composure. "I don't know what business you have barging in here and—"

"Thank you," Floyd interrupted, and dashed back outside.

Well, Floyd thought, *time to go make some trouble.*

....

First he found a supervillain's lair. By now, he wasn't too horribly surprised to find it emptied of its occupants, and he wasn't disappointed by the spoils of weaponry and equipment left behind. He picked out a high powered energy rifle, two or three weapons of unknown capabilities, and all the useful gadgetry he could conveniently carry. He rigged the doorway to some explosives, so that whenever the owner returned, the entire thing would detonate. Grinning maniacally, he stepped back out into the daylight.

London was waking up. People were stretching, yawning, scratching, and getting out of bed. They were climbing into clothes, tying shoe laces, and pouring milk over Lucky Charms. They were driving to work, honking at other people driving to work, and swearing at delays on bridges. They were setting into comfy office chairs behind desks that were either messy or meticulously organized. They were answering inane telephone calls and replying to idiotic emails. They read newspapers and saw that it was going to be a nice day. The temperature was 60 degrees, as usual, and it was going to rain. As usual. Crime rates were down, which was unusual, but no one was going to complain. They expected another day filled with drudgery and food and annoying people and cell phones and traffic.

They were not expecting Floyd to start shooting at trees.

He went back to the street where he'd fought Two-Face two nights earlier. There was a construction crew putting new glass into the department store window. They had scaffolding on the side of the building, and construction cones set up in the parking lane. Drivers weaved around them, occasionally honking and swearing.

He ran a hand over the barrel of his shiny new gun, still grinning like a lunatic. The trees were there too, exactly as he remember them, lined up at perfect intervals, in their equally sized square holes in the pavement. Floyd lowered the barrel of the rifle, took careful aim, and fired. Blue energy whipped through the air with a noise vaguely resembling thunder, hit the tree with a brief popping sound, and went up in smoke, taking half the branches away with it. Floyd aimed at the second tree and fired again.

He had covered two blocks before anyone really started to notice. He'd almost made it to three when he heard the sirens. Unlike the villains of two nights ago, he took that as his cue to disappear. He dropped the rifle and ran.

He heard shouts of "stop!", and he heard feet behind him, but mere policemen didn't stand a chance against him, and soon enough he was completely alone.

He slowed down to get his bearings and double check that he hadn't been followed. Then he pondered what sort of havoc to wreak next. A nice pub fight would be best, but he doubted he'd find anyone to brawl with at this time of day.

He found a nice roof to perch on and went through his gadgets. There was a supersonic emitter that did something terrible to cell phones. There was a heat sensor array. There was a cop detector, which was pretty nifty.

There were the two smaller weapons as well. Experimentation showed that they were energy powered as well. Floyd smiled. It was time to cause some real havoc.

The car dealership never even stood a chance. Floyd didn't even have to pull one of his shiny new guns; he had the car started and was gone before they could blink. He sped along as quickly as London traffic allowed, which wasn't very fast at all, but certainly reckless enough to cause a few minor bumps and bruises along the way. He laughed aloud and he kept his eyes peeled, and when he heard the cops coming, he jumped from the car and ran.

He ran across the highway, through the traffic, vaulting a few cars as he did so. He found himself in a residential area and took a shortcut through backyards to avoid detection. He came suddenly upon a grocery store, and dropped between the fence and the rubbish bins to collect his thoughts, catch his breath, and control his laughter. As he did so, he heard a small, tinny voice laughing beside him.

He turned and looked in astonishment. A hunchbacked midget was rolling back and forth on the ground, howling with laughter. Floyd waited just long enough to verify that he was a henchman and then he pounced.

"Who are you?" he shouted, shaking the midget. "Where are the villains?"

The henchman's laughter cut off abruptly and he stared in fear. Floyd changed his tactics to be more specific.

"I'm looking for Two-Face," he said threateningly. "Where is he?"

"Two-two-" the midget stammered.

"Where is he?" Floyd repeated fiercely.

"Gone," the midget wailed. "They're all gone."

"Gone where?"

"Gone. Goooooone..."

Floyd shook him harshly. "Gone where?" he shouted.

Sirens sounded nearby. The midget tried to dash away, but Floyd held him fast.

"Gone where?" he repeated.

"Away. Far away. In big airplanes, to the middle of nowhere..."

The midget wasn't making any sense. Disgusted, Floyd gave up, and turned to find himself running straight into the arms of a policeman.

They forced him to the ground, handcuffed him, and hauled him into the back of a squad car. It was then 8:45. By the time they reached the station, it was 9:00 exactly. Floyd was grinning.

The Chief Inspector walked in the door mere seconds before Floyd and his escort did.

"Inspector O'Rourke!" Floyd shouted. "I wanted to talk to you."

The Inspector paused. Floyd's escort paused. The Inspector looked at him, then at the report in his hand.

"An hour ago we had reports of someone shooting trees with an energy rifle on Park Boulevard," he said. "We thought it was a supervillain. Was it you?"

"Yes," Floyd admitted smugly.

"And the car theft twenty minutes later; was that you, too?"

"Yes, it was." Floyd tried to shrug out of the ungentle grip that held him immovable. "Can we talk, please?"

"Who on earth do you think you are?" the inspector asked in astonishment.

"Jeffry Floyd," Floyd said, sticking out his hand. Since it was handcuffed to the other one it rather lost the effect and was completely ignored. "At your service."

The chief inspector sighed and put a hand to his forehead, as though warding off a sudden pain there.

"Bring him back to my office," he said in resignation. "We'll talk."

Floyd finally succeeded in getting out of the grip of the officers on either side of him, who were more than a little stunned at their new orders. They said nothing, however, and escorted Floyd back to the office where the Chief Inspector was already waiting for them.

"Sit," he said, pointing with a ballpoint pen.

Floyd sat. The officers stood along the wall.

"What was all that about?" the inspector asked.

"What?" Floyd asked, feigning innocence.

"The trees and the car theft," the inspector said threateningly.

"Oh, that! I was trying to attract some attention."

"You wanted to get arrested?"

"No. I wanted a henchman."

"A henchman," Inspector O'Rourke said flatly.

"Yes," Floyd confirmed.

"And can you tell me why you needed a henchman?"

"To tell me where all the supervillains are."

"The supervillains?"

"Yes," Floyd said. "Big scary fellows causing havoc since last November?"

"What about them?"

"They're missing."

"Missing?"

"Look!" Floyd exclaimed, tired of the question and answer. "I checked with the night clerk, and there hasn't been a single crime committed all night. Where are they? What are they up to?"

"That's good news for us," the inspector said severely.

Floyd shook his head vehemently.

"And I don't see why you care," he added. "Go write a story about it for your paper or something."

"They're up to something," Floyd said ominously.

"And the longer they're up to it the better I like it," the inspector said. "Now I don't know what Inspector McCormick sees in you—"

"I'll tell you what he sees in me," Floyd interrupted. He stood, and his eyes darkened with deadly seriousness. "I see things most people don't see. I get things done. I capture supervillains. I defeat monsters. I do the things you're not capable of doing."

The Chief Inspector sighed and rubbed his forehead.

"Before I let you go with a warning notice and yet *another* mark on your record, you said there was something you wanted to talk about."

"Uh, yes." Floyd's confidence crumpled around him and he sat down. "It's about my friend, Joseph Adams."

"As I understand it, he's been suspended."

"Yes sir, that's what I wanted to talk to you about."

"It's a miracle," the inspector said sarcastically. "He's being respectful."

26

"It wasn't his fault," Floyd blurted out. "Those papers that were lost were taken by a supervillain named Two-Face, and I'm pretty sure he took them specifically to annoy me. Now if I can find him, I can find the papers, and Joseph doesn't have to come into this at all."

"Young man," the chief inspector said, leaning back and putting his finger tips together. "Joseph Adams was given a duty to safely deliver those papers, and he failed in that duty. The reason why he failed is immaterial."

"You don't understand," Floyd said. "I'm accepting responsibility."

"You can't do that."

"Why not?"

"Besides the fact that you don't even understand the meaning of the word?"

Floyd flushed angrily, but stayed silent.

"You're not a police officer," the inspector said. "You'll never be a police officer, no matter how many cases you 'consult' on. And this is a strictly departmental affair."

"But—"

"There's nothing more to be said about it. You may go, Mr. Floyd."

"It's not fair!" Floyd shouted, as the officers hauled him to his feet. "It wasn't his fault!"

The chief inspector paid him absolutely no mind as the officers hauled him back to the lobby, unlatched the handcuffs, and turned him loose outside.

Floyd picked himself up, straightened his coat, ran a hand through his hair, and decided to make a phone call.

CASUAL
ACQUAINTANCES
FOREVER

"Hello?"

"Joseph? This is Floyd."

"I seem to remember giving you very specific instructions never to call me at home, Floyd."

"Look. How do I usually get in touch with you?"

"You come to the station."

"Are you at the station?"

A pause. "No."

"Exactly. Do you know what happens when I go to the station and you aren't there? I get laughed at, physically assaulted, and thrown back out without getting the information I need."

Adams sighed. "That happens even when I am there, Floyd."

"That's beside the point."

"What do you want?"

"I was thinking, since you're not doing anything this weekend, maybe you would come with me on a little trip."

"Goodbye, Floyd."

"Wait, wait, hear me out!" he protested.

Adams sighed again. "What kind of trip?"

"Middle of nowhere," Floyd said promptly.

"Come again?"

"Middle of nowhere," Floyd said. "But my source was a bit unreliable, and considering the current state of supervillain-occupied-Africa, I'm going to guess it has to be somewhere more civilized."

"I don't follow."

"I want to take a trip to the Western United States."

There was a very long pause. "Come again?"

"I want to go to the United States," Floyd repeated impatiently. "The Western half of."

"Dare I ask why?"

"The supervillains are up to something. I don't know what and I don't know why and I don't like it."

"That sounds like every day to me."

"Joseph, they're leaving the country!"

"Why?"

"I don't know."

"What makes you think they're going to the United States?"

"A hunch."

"What is your hunch based on?"

"A hunchback midget henchman who was laughing at my escapades this morning."

Adams hesitated. "Escapades?"

"Forget I said that," Floyd said hastily. "The question is, are you coming or not?"

30

"I have a better question," Adams said irritably. "Are you going or not?"

"Come again?"

"Do you even have any means of getting out of this country?"

Floyd frowned. "I'm sure I do," he said hesitantly.

"I suggest you make sure you do," Adams said crossly. "And find a more solid reason for wanting to go on this wild goose chase."

The phone hung up with a sharp click. Floyd sighed. He couldn't remember if he had a passport or not, and he had no idea what he would have done with it if he had. He also was extremely uncertain how he would have obtained one in the first place.

There was nothing for it but to look. He took his laptop off the table, dumped it on the bed, and dug several cardboard boxes out of his closet. These he hauled back into the kitchen, and emptied out onto the now-clear table. There were photos and newspapers, letters, post cards, and junkmail, old forms and flyers and several different kinds of currency—all remnants of a life he had never really lived.

There was no identification.

He sat back and puzzled. Then he called Adams back.

"Hello?"

"This is Floyd. I figured it out."

"Figured what out?"

"It's a coalition."

"A what?"

"A temporary alliance between usually hostile parties to obtain a common and mutually beneficial goal."

"I don't follow."

"The supervillains are forming a coalition to obtain some mutually beneficial goal. And when I say mutually beneficial I mean beneficial to them, the supervillains, which spells disaster and devastation for the rest of us."

"That sounds serious."

"It is serious. Look, can you come over?"

"Floyd, I don't know..."

"Please?"

Adams sighed. "All right."

"Oh, thank you," Floyd cheered up instantly. "And pick up something for us to eat on your way over, would you? I'm starving."

....

Adams brought pizza.

"I hate pizza," Floyd said, slightly confused.

"I know," Adams said, with just the edge of a smile. "That's why I got it."

Floyd sighed and cleared a spot on the floor.

"I have a question," Adams said frankly, after poking around in Floyd's empty kitchen.

"What's that?"

"Do you eat at all when I'm not here?"

Floyd blinked. "I don't eat as much as you humans," he said uncertainly.

"Except when you're regenerating."

Floyd's face wrinkled with distaste. "Let's not talk about that."

"Fine. What is all over your table?"

"I was looking for my passport."

"Did you find it?"

"No. I don't think I have one."

"Don't think?"

"I don't remember."

"How can you not remember if you have a passport?" Adams demanded.

Floyd cringed, but he answered the question. "It was a really, really rough six months," he said vaguely.

Adams munched on a slice of pizza and waited for Floyd to continue.

"On earth," he tried to explain. "My first six months here. They were bad."

"You don't remember them?"

Floyd shook his head. "Not well. It's all a bit of a blur."

"Is earth really that bad?"

Floyd sighed. "The days are too long," he said softly. "It's too loud and too bright and there's too much gravity. There are too many people, and the buildings are too short. The food is all wrong, and too many things make me dizzy or sick. But after a while you get used to it. The wrongness becomes normal and you forget what normal really is..."

"I'm sorry," Adams said unexpectedly.

Floyd shook his head in dismissal. "I don't think I have a passport," he said, changing the subject back.

"How did you get into this country without a passport?" Adams demanded.

Floyd frowned in thought. "I think I stowed away on a freighter," he said.

Adams regretted the question. Floyd sprang to his feet with a look of pure devilry in his eyes.

"We're going to hitch a ride."

....

The bar was extremely loud and uncomfortably dim. The flashing, colored lights did nothing to illuminate the interior. A band on stage was singing a slow, pulsing rendition of "Even Supervillains Need a Little Bit of Fun." Women in scanty costumes danced with men who weren't quite normal.

Adams looked around uneasily. "I didn't know this place existed," he said in a low voice.

"And you're going to forget it exists," Floyd said, pushing his way through the apathetic crowd.

"There's a whole nest of crooks in here," Adams protested.

"Exactly," Floyd said. "Right where I can keep an eye on them."

"Floyd..."

"I'm not a police officer," Floyd said. "I'm not bound by your code of ethics."

"Well, I don't like it," Adams muttered.

"You'll get over it."

"Hey, Floyd!" someone shouted drunkenly. "What's the idea of bringing a copper here?"

"Mind your own business, Colin," Floyd said crossly.

"You trying to double-cross us? The boss doesn't like being double-crossed."

"I said shut up," Floyd snapped. "Or I'll pick you."

"Pick me for what?" Colin sneered. "What are you going to do, huh?"

"This," Floyd said, whirling on him. He grabbed Colin by his collar and tossed him onto the dance floor.

The music stopped abruptly, and the dancers cleared the area. Adams watched with interest.

"Oh, so you want to do that, do you?" Colin sneered. His skin was discolored, but there wasn't enough light to make out much more detail than that. He had light colored hair that fell over his eyes, and like most people in the world, he was several inches taller than Floyd.

He stood up and rubbed his hands together gleefully. Sparks leapt from between them.

"Come on," he said, dancing about the floor. "Come on, then."

Floyd folded his arms and pretended to be reluctant. "I don't want to do this," he said.

"Come on," Colin repeated eagerly.

"I want information," Floyd warned.

The silence in the room was tangible.

"So you're playing that card again," Colin snarled. He gathered himself together and rushed at Floyd, but by the time he got there, Floyd had moved. Floyd kicked him squarely in the back which combined with Colin's forward motion to send the villain sprawling to the ground. Floyd reached out, grabbed his shirt again, and tossed him back onto the dance floor. Before the villain could get himself back together, Floyd was standing over him with one foot on his neck, choking him.

"Start talking," Floyd said warningly.

The rest of the villains remained carefully uninvolved.

"Talk about what?" Colin gasped.

"Airports," Floyd said calmly.

"Airplanes leave airports," Colin said. "They go to other places."

"Yes," Floyd agreed.

"They take off and land on runways," Colin tried again.

"Tell me something I don't know," Floyd suggested.

"They're very popular these days?" Colin attempted.

Floyd just smiled.

"Hyena is leaving on one tomorrow," Colin said desperately. "From London Heathrow. He said something about a retreat… I don't know. He wants to calm his nerves or some such thing."

"Thank you," Floyd said, stepping back. "You've been most helpful."

"Floyd!" a new voice shouted. "I told you to never come back here!"

"Did you really?" Floyd said sarcastically. "I don't seem to remember getting that message."

"We've got something to settle, you and I." The new speaker was dark-skinned, dressed in black, and wearing sunglasses, which seemed strangely out of place in his surroundings.

"Of course we do," Floyd said patiently. "But I'm going out of town."

"What do you mean, out of town?" Colin frowned.

"I have a plane to catch," Floyd said, grinning. "Come on, Adams."

"Floyd," Adams said uncertainly.

"Floyd!" Colin shouted.

"Floyd!" the sunglass guy shouted.

Floyd grabbed Adams' arm and ran.

………

Heathrow airport is bright and shiny and loud and bustling and filled with people coming and going from all parts of the world. It was big enough and busy enough that very few people were actually affected by the hijacking of a jet bound for Switzerland. The people who were affected was the pilot, who ended up dead, the co-pilot, who died of his injuries four hours later in the hospital, and the 337 passengers who were unable to board their plane because it wasn't there when it was supposed to be. The flight control tower was slightly inconvenienced by a plane lifting off without clearance and promptly heading in the wrong direction, there was a baggage truck over turned and three planes whose landings were delayed until it could be cleaned up.

Four hours later, the hijacker was inconvenienced by being thrown out the window by another hijacker. He fell screaming to his death into the Atlantic ocean, and Floyd slid into the pilot's seat as though he belonged there. Adams watched him uneasily.

"Do you know how to fly?" he asked.

"Of course I know how to fly," Floyd retorted. "Have a seat."

"Was that in your supervillain training manual?"

"No, it's just common sense."

"I still don't feel right about this," the policeman confessed.

"You'll get over it," Floyd promised.

Adams sighed and sat in the co-pilot's seat. "How long until we get there?" he asked.

Floyd glanced at the chronometer. "An hour and a half," he said, "if all goes well."

"Are you sure you know what you're doing?" Adams pressed.

Floyd glanced sideways at his companion and grinned widely.

"Sure," he said. Adams wasn't convinced.

"Do you know where the supervillains are going?" he asked suspiciously.

Floyd shrugged. "Not really."

"Taking a stab in the dark?"

"That's right."

"Is that really going to work?" Adams said dubiously.

"I don't know," Floyd laughed. "I've never tried it before."

"Are you sure you don't have an ulterior motive?"

Floyd glanced at Adams and laughed again. "An ulterior motive?" he repeated. "No. What on earth would I do with one of those?"

"You're a terrible liar," Adams said, folding his arms.

"I'm not lying," Floyd retorted.

"What are you worried about?"

"Worried?" Floyd looked up with wide, innocent eyes. "Why would I be worried?"

"Oh, I don't know," Adams leaned back and gazed out the window. "I can think of a few things."

"Such as?"

"Such as maybe you don't really know how to fly."

Floyd laughed and shook his head. "I can fly," he said confidently. "You don't have to worry about that."

"I'm not the one having trouble keeping up a pretense of careless happiness," Adams said pointedly.

Floyd looked up to meet his gaze and didn't smile.

"See?" Adams said, vindicated. "So what are you worried about?"

"The US Military," Floyd admitted. "I've never dealt with military before."

"Well, here's a hint," Adams advised him. "Do exactly what they say and don't try to get smart."

Floyd looked back at the instrument panel.

"Why are you worried about them all of a sudden?" Adams asked.

"Because they've got two fighter jets on our tail."

"What?" Adams sat bolt upright. "Where?"

Floyd pointed.

"Have you tried contacting them?"

"They're not responding."

"Have they tried contacting you?"

"No."

"Maybe they're just passing through."

"No," Floyd shook his head. "They're definitely staying right on our tail."

"An escort then?"

"Escorts usually announce themselves."

"Well, it doesn't rule out the possibility of an escort. Where are we?"

"We'll be over New York in about ten minutes."

"Well, if they're going to get all nasty they'll do it before then," Adams said. "They won't shoot down a plane over a major city."

Floyd didn't reply.

"Would they?" Adams asked, suddenly alarmed.

Floyd shrugged. "I don't know. I've never dealt with military. I can't even be sure that they *are* military."

"Are you sure you know what you're getting into coming to this country?" Adams asked.

"I never know what I'm getting into," Floyd said.

"They're big superhero people," Adams told him.

Floyd swore under his breath.

"That's what I mean," Adams said nodding. "You won't like them at all. They have a government funded project poetically referred to as 'Assemble.' Not much has happened yet, or what has happened hasn't been publicized, but it's one of the biggest pet projects of the American people today."

"Great," Floyd said, rolling his eyes. "Just great."

"Have you made up your mind yet that this is all a terrible idea and that we should just go home?" Adams asked hopefully.

"Nope," Floyd grinned maniacally. "Not going anywhere except after those villains. I want to know what they're planning."

"You could leave it to the American Military," Adams suggested. "They seem efficient."

Floyd laughed and shook his head.

"Welcome to the United States," he said. "We're flying over New York and we're being asked to identify ourselves."

"Well, by all means, captain, identify yourself," Adams said.

Floyd grinned and radioed back.

"The name is Floyd, Jeffry Floyd. I'm here with Sergeant Adams and we're coming to investigate this Superhero Initiative I hear you've started."

He grinned at Adams who glared disapprovingly.

"What?" Floyd asked innocently.

"You were smart," Adams said. "I told you not to get smart with them."

"But it's so much fun!" Floyd protested.

"Sure," Adams agreed. "If getting killed is your idea of fun."

"Don't be paranoid," Floyd said. "Where's your sense of adventure and risk?"

He was cut off by a shudder that tore through the plane. The jets had opened fire.

"I told you so!" Adams shouted ungraciously over the sudden chaos.

"Shut up," Floyd snapped.

"You can't even fly," Adams added.

"I'll never be able to prove you wrong, will I?" Floyd argued. "I recall telling you to be quiet!"

The plane fell out of the sky in a fiery wreck.

WE'RE NOT IN KANSAS ANYMORE

They landed in the ocean.

The fighter jets wheeled off, their work done.

"Jump!" Floyd shouted to Adams, as the ground came up and the plane went down.

"Jump?" Adams repeated.

"It's water," Floyd said. "It will be all right."

"Easy for you to say," Adams argued.

"Listen to me," Floyd said intently, grabbing his arms. "You will be all right. I promise. Now get out of here before the whole thing explodes."

Adams glared, but Floyd pushed him, and they both fell into the Atlantic ocean.

A short while later a coast guard helicopter picked them up, gave them blankets and hot chocolate and kindly asked them what had happened.

Floyd opened his mouth and Adams smacked him.

"Our plane was hijacked by a supervillain," Adams explained.

Oh, that would explain it, the coast guard said, nodding. They apologized for the inconvenience, they asked where they were headed, they said if they needed anything to let them know, and to please enjoy their visit to the states.

"You hit me," Floyd complained, as they finally got underway again.

"I admit that I was wrong about your flying abilities," Adams said by way of apology.

"I can't believe they bought your line about the supervillains," Floyd said. "I could have come up with a much better story."

"They bought it because it was true," Adams said. "And it happens all the time. There's nothing suspicious there. As long as no one knows that you were the hijacker we're fine."

"I wasn't the original hijacker," Floyd tried to argue.

"Try explaining that," Adams said. "Or don't try explaining it and just leave well enough alone."

Floyd sighed and rubbed his eyes.

"Are you tired?" Adams asked.

Floyd shook his head. "I've been up for 48 hours tracking supervillains, stealing a plane, and crashing it in the Atlantic ocean," he said. "Why would I be tired?"

"Do you have a plan?" Adams asked.

"No," Floyd said. "I need Wi-Fi."

"Didn't your computer go down in the crash?"

Floyd just stared at Adams, who finally noticed the satchel he hadn't let go off all day.

"Of course it didn't," he clarified. "All right, so you need Wi-Fi. Anything else?"

"A drink," Floyd said quickly. "And I might need to make a phone call."

....

"This is not what I had in mind," Floyd said, staring up at the friendly green sign of the coffee shop.

Adams shrugged and walked ahead of him into the building. "It's warm and dry," he said. "And they have coffee. And free Wi-Fi."

Given no other choice, Floyd followed him in. He was right about it being warm, too warm in fact. He shrugged out of his coat and then set his laptop on the table. Adams came over a few minutes later carrying two Styrofoam mugs. Floyd glared at them suspiciously.

"You know I don't drink coffee," he said accusingly.

"Relax," Adams said. "Yours is orange juice."

Obediently, Floyd relaxed. He sipped his orange juice absently while searching for the information he needed. Adams sat back and enjoyed the peaceful quiet for as long as it would last, which wasn't very long at all.

"Find something?" Adams inquired casually.

"We need to go west," Floyd said.

Adams tried not to look incredulous.

"Kansas," Floyd said impatiently. "We need to get to Kansas. Can we take a train from here?"

Adams sighed and finished his coffee. "I'll find out," he said.

He came back half an hour later with two bus tickets instead, and found Floyd fast asleep, leaning against the window.

"Hey kid," he said, shaking him awake. "You can sleep on the bus."

Floyd sat up with a startled gasp, his eyes filled with raw panic.

"Hey, take it easy," Adams said, stepping back and raising his hands in surrender. "It's just me."

Floyd's eyes darted around the room, but he seemed to relax.

"You wanted to go to Kansas," Adams said, "so I got us tickets to Kansas. You ready to go?"

Floyd nodded and started to gather up his things, but his hands were shaking so badly he could barely control them. Adams took everything away from him and packed it for him.

"When was the last time you ate?" he asked.

"When was the last time *you* ate?" Floyd retorted.

"Come on," Adams said, slinging Floyd's satchel over one shoulder. He put his other hand under Floyd's elbow and pulled him to his feet. "We'll get something at the bus station."

Floyd went along compliantly and didn't say another word. Adams bought peanuts and hotdogs, found their seats, put Floyd next to the window, and made him eat. By the time they pulled out of the station, Floyd was asleep again. Adams began to hope that this would be a very uneventful trip.

Floyd slept for an astonishing eight hours. He woke up starving, ate what was left of the peanuts, stared out the window for five minutes, and then decided he was bored.

"Where are we?"

Adams consulted a map.

"Illinois."

46

"How long until we get there?"

"Not for another twelve hours."

"How big is this country?"

Adams fixed him with a glare.

Floyd shrugged. "I'm just curious," he said. "It seems to take forever to get anywhere."

"Big," Adams said flatly. "Any chance you're going to go back to sleep?"

Floyd grinned in amusement. "None."

Adams didn't reply. There was a moment of respite.

"How big?"

Adams swore. "Do I look like a walking encyclopedia?"

Floyd went back to staring out the window. He almost managed to stay quiet for ten minutes before turning impatiently to Adams.

"Are you sure you don't know—" he started, but dropped off when he saw the steely look in his friend's eyes. He sighed and looked back at the window.

In the seat in front of them a friendly, elderly gentleman put down his newspaper and glanced back.

"You're not from around here, are you?" he commented.

Floyd shook his head. "No," he agreed. "I'm quite a ways from home."

"Where is home?" the gentleman inquired.

"Right now it's in London," Floyd said cheerfully.

"Ever been to the states before?"

Floyd thought a minute. "Yes," he said finally. "I think so. It seems like a lifetime ago."

"So what's bringing you back then?"

"I'm looking up an old acquaintance," Floyd said with a grin. "Say, do you know—"

"Yes, I heard you ask your friend," the gentleman chuckled. "He gave you the right answer, you know. It's a big country."

"It's a big world," Floyd retorted.

"Yes, I suppose it is," the gentleman agreed. "But then, the entire universe is a big place."

Floyd snorted with laughter. "You have no idea."

The gentleman raised his eyebrows politely. "Excuse me?"

"I mean," Floyd clarified hastily, "we have no idea. What's out there. It's a big, big place."

"Floyd," Adams said sharply.

The gentleman shifted his attention from Floyd to the police officer.

"What's your story?" he asked.

Adams' look was one of patient resignation. "I'm the one with the money," he said calmly.

"Hey!" Floyd protested.

"Didn't think of that, did you?" Adams said smugly.

Floyd folded his arms and glared. The bus rumbled to a stop.

Floyd was on his feet in a second. "Are we arrived?" he asked eagerly.

"No," Adams shook his head. "It's just another stop along the way."

Crestfallen, Floyd sat back down again.

"It'll be at least half an hour before we get going again," the gentleman said. "You could go look around."

Floyd stood up again.

"I don't think that's a good idea," Adams said.

Floyd glanced down at him. "Please?" he said simply.

Adams sighed.

"How much trouble can he get into?" the gentleman said encouragingly.

"You'd be surprised," Adams muttered. He tossed aside the pamphlet he'd been pretending to read and stood up.

"Come on then," he said.

Floyd looked surprised.

"I'm not letting you out there on your own," Adams said pointedly. "Come on."

The gentleman settled back with his newspaper and smiled at them as they walked out. "Have fun," he said encouragingly.

The bus station was busy and bustling with people. Floyd looked around and grinned.

"What's the real reason we're here?" Adams asked, following him through the crowd.

"I told you," Floyd said. "We're looking for a coalition."

"There is no coalition, Floyd."

"Sure there is!" he said in surprise.

"Where are you getting your information?"

Floyd shrugged. "Here and there," he said. "Rumors, reports... there's tracking data for this stuff, you know."

"Tracking data?" Adams said incredulously. "For supervillains?"

"Amazing what they come up with, isn't it?" Floyd grinned. "This country is huge, Joseph. How do they deal with the villains here, I wonder?"

"They're Americans," Adams said dryly. "How do they deal with anything?"

Floyd stared blankly.

"I forgot you didn't know basic history," Adams said. "Never mind."

Floyd glanced back in surprise, forgetting to look where he was going as he did so.

"Hey, pal, watch where you're going!"

"Sorry," Floyd apologized immediately, looking to see who he'd run into, and froze in recognition.

The weasely little man in front of him was short, almost shorter than Floyd. He was bald and he carried a brief case and he sneered up at them.

"Don't I know you?" Floyd said, frowning.

"I don't think so, paley. You don't look like my type."

The man started to walk off, but Floyd grabbed his arm and stared.

"I know you," he repeated.

The stranger looked intently at Floyd's hand on his arm. "Take your hands off me," he said. "That's assault, you know."

"Floyd," Adams said warningly.

"London, England, Sixteenth Street, fourteenth February, one-thirty AM," Floyd rattled off quickly.

The weasel-faced man looked uncomfortable. "You've got me mixed up," he said.

"Girl named Terra," Floyd continued, remembering. "Nice girl. Red blouse. Told you I never wanted to see your face again."

"And you wouldn't have," the man sneered, "if you'd stayed in your own part of the world."

He tried to walk off, but Floyd twisted his arm, sending him spinning back into the crowd. There was a collective gasp and people started to move away.

"Floyd," Adams said commandingly.

The weasel-faced man picked himself up off the ground, his sneer melting into rage.

"You want to get ugly?" he yelled. "Let's make this ugly then."

"Walk away, Floyd," Adams said. He put his hand on Floyd's shoulder and the alien whirled around, his eyes smoldering in dark anger.

"I know who this is," he said intently.

"You'd better listen to your handler," Weasel called back at him.

"Walk away," Adams repeated. "If you get into a fight here and thrown into an American prison I'm not coming to visit you."

"You'd leave me here?" Floyd said incredulously.

"I will go back to England without you," Adams said. "And good luck finding another officer to be as lenient with you as I have been."

Floyd glanced back. Weasel spread his hands, waiting. There was a disturbance further down.

"That's the police now," Adams said. "Are you coming with me or not?"

Floyd hesitated. Adams waited. Weasel grinned.

"I'm not done with you yet," Floyd said, pointing at the villain. "This isn't over!"

"I'll be waiting for you," Weasel said, pleased with himself.

Floyd darted off, struggling to keep up with Adams as he walked through the crowd back to the bus.

"Idiot," Adams said, without turning around.

"I know who he is," Floyd defended himself.

"You're still an idiot," Adams said.

"It's not like what I do is legal in England," Floyd protested.

"At least you have a home and a job there," Adams said. "You really want to go on the run in a new place?"

Floyd shrugged. "What difference does it make?" he asked.

Adams whirled around and looked at him. "You tell me," he said. "Why did you settle in England?"

Floyd shrugged. Adams kept walking.

"You pull another stunt like that and I'm done," Adams said. "I'm only here because I had nothing else to do, and I have no interest in getting into even more trouble than I already am."

He climbed on board, showed the driver their tickets and headed back to their seats.

"I have no intention of being arrested," Floyd argued.

"I'm sure you never intend to do it," Adams said, "but it sure happens an awful lot."

Floyd opened his mouth and shut it again. The gentleman in front of them looked up and raised his eyebrows in understanding.

"I told you so," Adams snapped.

"Sit," he said to Floyd.

Floyd sat, folded his arms defiantly, and glared out the window again. Adams unfolded the newspaper he'd picked up in the station and ignored him. Five minutes later, the bus pulled out.

The sun was setting on another day. Miles of flat farmland rolled away on either side of the highway. Traffic became less frequent. Adams finished his paper and realized in some surprise that Floyd hadn't bothered him in quite some time. He glanced sideways at his companion. Floyd was asleep.

This was unusual, but since a sleeping Floyd was significantly less trouble than an awake one, he left him alone. Gradually, it got darker. Eventually, Adams dozed off as well.

He was awakened some time later by the bus coming to a halt. He looked around, momentarily confused about where he was. Softly murmuring voices indicated that the other passengers were confused as well. There was no sound from the driver.

Adams had just decided that it was probably a flat tire or something and settled back again when there was a banging at the door and a rough voice ordered everyone out.

The murmur began to rise in pitch and Adams realized that the situation could get very bad very fast. He woke Floyd up.

The rough voice repeated the command. It sounded somewhat muffled, Adams thought, as though the speaker was wearing a mask over his face. He shook Floyd again. People started to get up and move towards the exit.

It was too dark to make out details. A lot of people were still unaware of what was going on. Adams frowned at his unresponsive companion.

"Floyd, you've got to wake up," he whispered harshly. Floyd mumbled something unintelligible and didn't open his eyes. The gentleman with the newspaper looked back at them, his eyes wide with sleep and confusion.

"Do you know what's going on?" he asked. Adams shook his head.

"It doesn't sound good," he confided.

"Everyone out of the bus!" the voice repeated. "Get a move on now."

Adams shook Floyd again, and then drew his hand back and slapped him.

Floyd jerked awake. "What's going on?" he asked in a voice that was too loud for the circumstances. His voice sparked a flood of conversation and broke the spell of quiet confusion that had lingered as a result of the late hour.

"What's going on?" people asked each other, looking around.

"Come on," Adams hissed, pulling Floyd to his feet. "Let's go see what this is all about."

Floyd let himself be led along, still confused.

"What's wrong with you?" Adams asked. "Snap out of it."

"Nothing's wrong with me," Floyd protested sleepily.

"You slept," Adams said. "Again."

"So?"

Adams sighed. As they got towards the front of the bus, he made out who it was standing in the shadows shouting at them. He was dressed completely in black and wearing a black ski mask. Definitely not good.

The night air was chill. The sky was crystal clear and strewn with stars. It was a breathtaking sight, but no one was looking. Their attention was focused in fear and bewilderment at the circle of men wearing ski masks and pointing guns at them.

A woman started crying. A man raised his voice belligerently. Floyd let go of Adams to rub his eyes and almost fell.

"Hey," Adams said, catching his arm. "Breathe."

To his surprise, Floyd obeyed.

"Who are all these guys?" he asked in a low voice.

"I don't know," Adams said calmly.

"What do they want?"

"I don't know that either."

"They could be henchmen," Floyd observed.

"Really?" Adams said dryly.

Floyd ignored the sarcasm in his voice. "Henchmen are notoriously underpaid," he said. "And some of them are surprisingly sane, considering the hight rate of insanity accompanying superpowers. They pull side jobs on their own sometimes."

"Mmm," Adams said. A masked man went around with a bag, collecting wallets and jewelry. Several woman screamed. A man protested and the henchman hit him. Another woman had hysterics. Floyd took his coat off and handed it to Adams.

"No," the policeman said. Floyd followed the predictable course of action and ignored him.

"Hey you," he said, walking towards the henchman doing the collecting. "Yeah, you. I'm talking to you."

If the henchman sneered, he couldn't tell because he was wearing a mask.

"What are you harassing these people for?" Floyd asked innocently.

"Hand over your wallet, kid, and get back," the henchman said.

"I haven't got any money," Floyd said, shaking his head.

"Is that so?" This time the sneer was evident in his voice. "Let's see what's in the bag of yours, then."

He held up a hand and another henchman came over.

"Hold this one down while I search him," the first henchman said.

"Gladly," the second one said.

Floyd waited until the last second before he dropped the act of surprised fear and turned on his attackers. He knocked down the second henchman and took his gun. He used it as a club and knocked the first one out cold. He turned on the rest of them and fired. The remainder scattered and vanished into the night. Floyd tossed the gun aside, turned back to the crowd and grinned.

He was met with stony glares.

Confused he picked up the bag the first henchman had dropped and tossed it to the bus driver.

"Everything's fine," he reassured them. "They won't be back any time soon."

"Show-off vigilante," the driver muttered. "Come on, everyone back on board."

Floyd sauntered over to Adams.

"Not the reception you expected?" Adams asked.

"No, not exactly," Floyd agreed. "I wonder what's eating them."

They found out when they tried to re-board the bus.

"You with him?" the driver asked, pointing first at Adams and then at Floyd.

"Yes," Adams said. "We're traveling together."

"Well you can stay with him, too," the driver said, shutting the doors.

"Hey," Floyd protested, catching the glass before it closed. "What's the idea?"

"I don't want no vigilante on my bus," the driver said. "And the passengers feel the same."

"Vigilante?" Floyd said. "I don't know what you're talking about."

"Don't play that game with me, young man. It won't do you no good."

"Hey," Floyd said angrily, but Adams put a hand out and stopped him.

"We're strangers here," Adams said. "We're just here visiting from England. I'm sorry, but we really don't know what you mean..."

"Your friend here is trouble," the driver said. "We don't want him around."

"I kept you from getting robbed!" Floyd exclaimed. "Possibly killed!"

"Maybe so, but you're trouble."

The driver shut the door firmly, terminating the conversation. Floyd started forward but Adams caught his arm and held him back.

"They're going to leave us here!" Floyd exclaimed.

"And there's nothing we can do about it," Adams said.

The bus started up and lumbered down the highway.

OH WAIT, YES WE ARE

5

"Well," Adams said.

Floyd threw up his hands in exasperation and then sat down on the road and stared moodily into the distance. "Now what?" he asked.

Adams sat down next to him. "I don't know," he said. "This isn't my trip."

"I wasn't intending to get kicked off the bus halfway to nowhere," Floyd said bitterly.

"That is a bit strange," Adams acknowledged.

"More than a bit," Floyd muttered. "Even granting that I'm trouble, people usually prefer being rescued to being robbed."

"Indeed," Adams said. "You admit to being trouble?" he added suddenly.

Floyd shrugged. "Sometimes, maybe."

"Hey," Adams said, suddenly remembering. "Are you all right?"

"Sure," Floyd said, puzzled. "Why wouldn't I be?"

"I don't know... you fell asleep."

"So?"

"So... it's just unusual, that's all."

"I must have been more tired than I expected."

"Mm," Adams said noncommittally.

Floyd laughed. "You don't need to worry about me," he said lightly.

"It's better than worrying about—" Adams stopped abruptly.

Floyd watched him in concern for a moment.

"Why worry about anything?" he asked finally. "It's a beautiful morning. The sun will be rising soon, and some passing traveler will take pity on a couple of foreigners stranded in the middle of nowhere..."

"How do we explain why we're stranded?"

Floyd grinned. "Who said we'll need an explanation?"

He stretched out and put his hands behind his head, staring up at the sky.

"Beautiful, isn't it?" Adams said beside him.

"Alien," Floyd retorted.

"What, the sky didn't look like this back home?"

"Nope."

"Tell me about it."

Floyd hesitated. "There were more stars," he said softly. "Much more. And they hung together in clusters that looked almost like they were ready to fall out of the sky. You could almost see them move, sometimes... and the higher you went the brighter they became. Less atmosphere."

"How did you breathe?" Adams asked, "if you went that high?"

Floyd laughed gently. "You didn't need to breathe," he said. "If you were that high, the stars would take your breath away... you couldn't stay long, of course. Just long enough to kiss a girl..."

"It sounds beautiful."

"It was breathtaking."

Adams had no reply to that.

"Tell me about them," Floyd said abruptly. "Your stars. What do you know about them?"

"Oh, not much," Adams said reluctantly. "I don't really know anything about astronomy."

"Tell me what you do know."

"They're very far away," Adams ventured, "And you're from one of them."

A genuine laugh from Floyd was a rare thing, and in the dark Adams smiled.

"It's nothing like your home, is it."

"You have a very nice planet," Floyd said politely.

Adams laughed. "But?"

"I like England better."

"And why is that?"

"I don't know. But I'm sure I'll figure it out."

"Do you remember being here before?"

"I was never here."

"In the country, I mean."

"I don't know. I would have to be there again, and this isn't it."

Another long pause.

"I don't think I've ever been stuck talking to you for this long," Adams commented.

Floyd snorted in amusement. "That makes two of us."

"Do you have a plan?"

"I never have a plan."

"Oh, that's right," Adams muttered. "You never have a plan."

"Hey," Floyd said warningly. "It's easier that way."

"According to you."

"Do you have a plan?"

"Yes. Go back to London and try to forget this whole thing ever happened."

"That bad, huh?"

"Oh yes."

Gradually the sky began to lighten.

"So why did you come?"

"Hm?"

"Why did you agree to come with me to the United States?"

"I didn't agree to come. You dragged me along."

"You came willingly. I invited you, and you followed. You could have turned around and left, and you didn't."

"Well... I was curious."

"Is that all?"

"I also had nothing better to do."

"I see."

"If I had left you, would you have come by yourself?"

"I don't know. Probably not."

"So this isn't about the coalition."

"This is about the coalition."

"Don't you have to stop them at any cost?"

"Yes..."

"So why is it personally related to me?"

Floyd sat up and glared at his companion. "Nothing is personally related to anyone," he said pointedly. "You just happen to be the only person in this entire world that I know can actually help me out in situations like this."

"You mean, I pay your expenses," Adams corrected.

"I wouldn't put it that way."

"You know it's true, though."

"If you weren't such a stickler for turning in everything we take from the lairs we wouldn't have to worry about expenses."

"Withholding evidence is illegal."

"How is it evidence?"

"You know the answer to that."

"It still doesn't make sense."

"It doesn't have to make sense. It's the law."

"Oh, have it your way."

"I do."

Floyd had no answer to that, so he shut up. For a few minutes.

"Did I ever mention that the days here are very long?"

"This isn't a day, Floyd. This is called night. That's why it's dark."

"Long night."

"Especially when you're stuck on a highway in the middle of nowhere with an alien in a bad mood."

"I'm not in a bad mood."

"You are."

"Joseph..."

"Just shut up, okay?"

"Okay," Floyd said, bewildered at the sudden shift in mood.

The sky lightened and the stars faded out, and Floyd stood up and began to pace restlessly.

"Headlights," Floyd said.

"Mmm?" Adams said.

"Get up," Floyd said, poking him with his foot. "Someone's coming."

Adams sat up and looked around. Sure enough, twin headlights were coming down the highway at a nice clip. Floyd waved his hands above his head.

To Adams' relief, the driver slowed and stopped beside them. It was a beat-up pickup truck that may have once been red, and the window rolled down to reveal a grizzled farmer.

"Do you need a ride?" he asked.

"Yes," Floyd said, interrupting Adams before the latter could speak. "We're travelers, you see, and we're a bit stranded..."

The farmer chewed for a moment. "Where are you headed?"

"Nowhere in particular," Floyd grinned.

"Somewhere with Wi-Fi and coffee," Adams corrected, glaring at Floyd.

"You're not from these parts, are you," the farmer observed.

"Nice deduction," Floyd said wryly.

"Be nice, Floyd," Adams said, elbowing him.

"Hop in," the farmer said. "I can take you as far as Middle-of-Nowhere."

Adams looked at Floyd and raised his eyebrows. Floyd simply walked around to the other side of the truck, opened the door, and hopped in. Adams followed.

"Name's Riley," the farmer said, sticking out a hand as he put the truck in gear.

"Floyd," Floyd said, shaking it. "This is Joseph Adams."

"What brings you all the way out here?"

"I'm looking for someone."

"Aaah," the farmer said in understanding. "Quite a few of those these days. The supervillains misplaced a lot of relatives."

64

"Do you have many supervillains here?" Floyd asked casually.

The farmer shrugged. "They're a pest like anything else," he said. "They come and go. We deal with them as best as we can."

"I see," Floyd said, not seeing at all.

"This is where it all began, you know," Riley volunteered. "They say it's different because of that but I've never seen it myself. Seems just like any other town I've been to."

"Wait a minute," Floyd said, excited. "When you say you can take us to middle-of-nowhere, you mean the Middle-of-Nowhere? The town where the first attack occurred?"

"That's right, young man."

"Wait," Adams interjected. "You mean there's an actual town named Middle-of-Nowhere?"

Floyd and Riley nodded seriously.

"I thought you just couldn't remember the name," Adams muttered. "Who would name a town that?"

"It's sad what happened there," Riley said. "They have quite a bit of tourists come by now, but really, the place has been pretty much torn apart."

"Any villains left?" Floyd asked.

"No, not that I know of anyway. I just go in for supplies every so often. My ranch is way back there."

Floyd nodded semi-intelligently.

"Villains are always worse in the city you know," the farmer continued. "All those people in one place. Out here... it's not worth their while. There's not any wealth, and very little trouble... you'd have to travel about thirty miles just to find something to smash properly. Oh, they crop up often enough, but they don't stay around. It's too peaceful."

"I'll remember that," Floyd said gravely.

"Your cover story is falling apart," Adams commented.

"It's not a cover story," Floyd said hotly.

"Who are you looking for again?" Riley said, skillfully diverting an awkward conversation.

"An old friend," Floyd said. "He disappeared unexpectedly a few weeks ago, but I heard that he might be in this part of the country."

"Hiding out, eh?"

"I don't know."

"I guess you're hoping you find him still human?"

"I'm afraid that's not likely," Floyd said.

"Well, you can't give up hope," Riley said philosophically. "Where did you say you were from?"

"London."

"Whereabouts be that? You've got to help me out, young man. I don't know every city in the world."

"England," Floyd said courteously.

"Seriously?" the farmer turned his head to stare at them. "No wonder you seemed like foreigners."

"We are," Floyd said.

"So you are. That's a long way to come looking for a missing friend."

"It's important," Floyd said, glancing at Adams.

"I guess so. He mean a lot to you?"

"He saved my life once or twice."

Riley whistled. "Friends like that are rare."

"So I've been told."

The sun was rising and began to shine brightly through the driver's window.

"What time is it?" Adams asked.

"6:45," the farmer offered. "We'll be there at seven exactly."

The town, as they drove through it, was indeed a mess. Buildings had been smashed and never rebuilt. Bits of debris still stuck through roofs on unfortunate buildings. No one was out and about this early. Riley pulled up in front of the courthouse, or what remained of it.

"Anywhere in particular you want to be dropped off?"

"No," Adams said. "This will do just fine."

"Thank you," Floyd added, clambering out after the policeman. "I appreciate it."

"Good luck finding your friend," Riley added.

Floyd waved enthusiastically as he drove off and then looked around with undisguised glee.

"I can't believe this," he said, shielding his eyes. "I've been wanting to come here forever. I mean, this is where it started!"

"So?" Adams asked unenthusiastically.

"Mayor Phillip Sanders was unexpectedly revealed to be a first class supervillain on 16th November, 2012," Floyd said formally.

"You sound like a reporter," Adams commented.

Floyd ignored him. "His powers included telekinesis and energy control. The real surprise was that his secretary turned out to be a villain as well. Ms. Scarlett Jones. Magnetic force and personal defense. In fact, no one is really sure which one developed first because they were both keeping their powers concealed, but they couldn't hide them from each other. The tension eventually escalated into a battle which destroyed both of them.

"Spontaneous supervillain outbreaks are extremely uncommon, and so there is definitely some question about whether or not either of them were truly the first. There is no way to know if, in some dark vault somewhere, genetic experimentations were being conducted, resulting in the first supervillain, and that it was the resulting ripples from that which infected both Mayor Sanders and Ms. Jones. If this is in fact the case, then it is more likely that the lab is quite close to this location, but so far no proof has been offered that these two were not indeed the very first villains."

"You sound like an encyclopedia," Adams said unappreciatively.

"If the true site of the origin of supervillains could be located, then we would be one step closer to figuring out what causes this phenomena. Unfortunately, most planets' outbreaks are untraceable. Earth has the cleanest beginning aside from Beta 65, but even that origin is a question in debate, and no proper research has been done on the subject."

"Are you done yet?" Adams asked, folding his arms.

Floyd blinked. "I suppose so," he said, looking around. "This is very exciting for me, you know."

"I gathered as much."

"The very first supervillain battle on Earth."

"Yes, that's what you said."

"Mayor Phillip Sanders—"

"Floyd!"

"—and Ms. Scarlett Jones..."

68

"You said that already."

"I did?" Floyd was confused. Adams took his arm, led him to a shady spot of the ruined courthouse, and made him sit down.

"What are we doing here?" he asked.

Floyd shook his head. "Is it very warm?" he asked.

Adams looked around and shrugged. "Not overly so," he said. "Are you all right?"

"We're looking for the coalition," Floyd said, answering the first question and ignoring the second. "They're around here somewhere. Planning something. It makes sense that they'd come back to where it all began. They're probably drawn here.

"There's a popular theory that supervillain outbreaks coincide with a rise in the percentage of a certain type of energy. No one has ever identified this energy or proven its existence, but gene alternations do seem to induce a spike. This is what causes the first supervillain to emerge. It's a vicious cycle where having more supervillains creates more energy, which in turn creates more villains until it's spread around the world. It continues to increase exponentially, but like any large system it eventually gets too big and it collapses. All the supervillains burn out, and the energy dissipates and returns to normal levels."

"Floyd," Adams said, shaking him. "Why are you talking so much?"

"There's a theory that if one could induce a surge in that energy it would burn out all the supervillains prematurely and end the attack... but it's never been proven. None of it has ever been proven. The energy might not exist. It might be something else entirely. There's another theory that they communicate subconsciously on a telepathic level and that it's all tied together by some kind of mental enhancement..."

"Floyd," Adams said. "Come on, Floyd. Focus. What's going on here?"

"Nothing," Floyd said. "Nothing at all. It's just history. No supervillains left. They don't hang around where they originated, you know. Too many ghosts. Do you believe in ghosts, Joseph?"

"No, I don't."

"Pity. They're real, you know. We should come back after dark and see them. Of course, some scientists say that they're really just an energy footprint left by the burnout... but that hasn't happened yet, has it? There hasn't been a burnout. And it's just a theory anyway. Probably isn't true at all."

Floyd stopped talking suddenly and looked up at Adams. "Is it very warm?" he asked.

Before Adams could answer his question for the second time, a new voice piped up.

"You certainly know a lot about supervillains," the new voice said. "Where do you get all this information?"

Floyd looked up, blinked, and shaded his eyes.

"Internet," he answered. "I have a website."

The newcomer was teenager in black jeans and a navy blue t-shirt. His hair was dark auburn and flopped into his eyes. He was ruggedly built, wore sturdy leather boots caked with mud, and had permanent callouses on his hands.

"Do you really?" he said, sauntering over. "What's it called?"

"Supervillain of the Day," Floyd said. He stuck out his hand. "My name's Floyd. What's yours?"

"Roger," the kid said. "Say, I know that name. I think I've seen your website before. What's your last name?"

"Floyd is my last name," Floyd said. "My first name is Jeffry."

Roger grinned. "Yup, that's you all right," he said. "I'm a big fan of your work. You've done some pretty good research. Say, isn't this a little far from your usual territory?"

"You've heard of me?" Floyd said.

"Yeah. Like I said, great work. But what are you doing here?"

"I'm looking for someone. Maybe you can help. If you keep up with local villains..."

"Sure do," Roger beamed. "Who can I help you find?"

Floyd glanced at Adams and then back up at Rogers. "Can we go someplace cooler?" he asked abruptly. "I'm having a hard time focusing..."

"Uh, sure," Roger said, glancing around. "I think the coffee shop will be open by now. We can go there."

"That sounds great," Adams said, standing up.

Roger saw him for the first time. "Who are you?" he asked bluntly.

"I'm the guy who keeps him alive," Adams said. "Come on, Floyd. Let's go."

HEAT WAVE

Adams made Floyd sit in a dark corner next to the air vent and brought him a glass of ice water and he seemed to relax some. Roger sat across from them as though he'd been invited, which Adams was careful to point out that he hadn't been.

"What's wrong?" he asked cheerfully.

"Nothing is wrong," Floyd said crossly. "What were we talking about?"

"You said it was hot," Roger offered.

"Before that," Floyd snapped.

"No need to get all irritable," Adams interjected. "You were talking about supervillains, Floyd. What else?"

"That's right," Floyd said, smiling. "You said you were familiar with my website. I'm flattered."

"Oh yeah," the kid said. "Like I said. You've done your research."

"I was well taught," Floyd said automatically.

"Interesting," Roger said. "Who taught you?"

"That's classified," Floyd said tautly.

73

"Hmm," Roger said dismissively. "I wouldn't have thought that the supervillains had been around long enough for someone to learn all that and teach it to someone else."

"It wasn't a person," Floyd said. "It was a computer. And the world is a much larger place than you suspect."

"I suggest you listen to him," Adams said. "He knows what he's talking about."

"And what are you?" Roger asked insolently. "His parole officer?"

Floyd and Adams exchanged glances. "Never mind that," Floyd said. "Can you help me?"

"What do you need help with if you know so much?"

"I'm looking for someone," Floyd said, getting out his laptop. "I want to know if you've seen him."

"Must be pretty important, huh?"

"It's very important," Floyd said. "Or I wouldn't be here."

"You didn't just come to see the place?"

Floyd shook his head. "It's just a bunch of ruins," he said dismissively. "Not much to see."

"That's not what you said ten minutes ago," Adams reminded him.

"Can't hold me to anything I said ten minutes ago," Floyd said.

"Why not?"

"I can't take the heat."

"It's not that hot," Roger snorted.

Floyd raised his eyebrows. "It is to me."

"Is that why you came to England?" Adams asked.

"I don't like sunshine," Floyd confirmed. He turned his computer so Rogers could take a look at it. "Seen that guy?"

"I... no. I don't think so."

"Okay... what about that one?"

"No. Definitely not."

"That one?"

"That's a maybe."

"Do you even have supervillains around here?"

Roger shrugged. "They turn up on occasion. Usually just passing through. We keep them in check, though."

"How do you do that?"

Rogers looked around. There was no one else in the entire room, but he leaned forward and lowered his voice anyway.

"Me and some of my buddies take care of them," he said. "They call us vigilantes, but all we want to do is keep everyone safe, see? We work together, and we've got ways of dealing with villains. We get a lot of useful information off your site. Like I said, you're good."

"Thanks," Floyd said, but his eyes said he didn't mean it. "Vigilantes?"

"People around here are a bit suspicious," Roger said. "You might not want to let them know who you are."

"I'll take that under consideration," Floyd said with mock gravity. "Tell me something, Roger."

"Sure."

"If you were dealing with supervillains on a global scale, how would you go about it?"

Roger whistled in surprise. "Is that your game?" he asked in an awed tone.

"Hypothetically," Floyd said warningly.

"Sure. Well, I'd create a network, that's what I'd do. I'd get people all over the world to start groups just like mine dedicated to taking out supervillains. I'd instate free exchange of information, and convince people to tell their friends to report any supervillain sightings. They've got some of that already, you know, but I'd make sure we could tap into that data. Maybe get a programming team on board to take care of the coding."

Floyd nodded. "So what if the supervillains caught onto you and joined forces?"

"Supervillains don't work together," Roger said, laughing at him. "It's against their nature."

"It's been known to happen."

"When?"

Floyd raised his eyebrows. "That's classified."

"Is it really?" Roger sneered. "Just who do you work for?"

"That's classified."

"You some kind of government agent?"

"Whatever you're thinking, you're wrong."

"Oh yeah? Well how do you know what I'm thinking? Are you some kind of telepath?"

Floyd didn't answer.

"Maybe you're the supervillain, eh?"

"The supervillains are forming a coalition," Floyd said, abruptly changing the subject. "I think their base is somewhere very near here. I'm trying to find it. I'm offering you a chance to help."

Roger stared, and then burst out laughing. "A coalition?" he exclaimed. "How naive are you? I just told you, villains don't work together."

"Not usually," Floyd sad patiently. "But they are this time."

"Are they?" Roger kept laughing. "And how do you know that?"

"They told me," Floyd said matter-of-factly.

"Man, supervillains don't talk to anyone," Roger said.

"They talk to me."

"Why would they do that?"

Floyd looked annoyed.

"No," Adams said quickly.

"He's asking for it," Floyd said.

"No," Adams repeated.

Rogers glanced between them, his hilarity curtailed. "What are you two talking about?" he asked uncertainly.

"Thank you for your help, Roger," Floyd said formally. "I'll be in touch."

"How can you be in touch if you don't how to get a hold of me?"

Floyd's stare made him feel uneasy this time.

"Don't ask that question," Adams suggested.

Rogers went, trying to collect his previous cocky attitude as he did so.

"He was asking for it," Floyd repeated, glaring at the young man as he left.

"Let it go, Floyd," Adams said. "You don't need to go around picking fights just to prove a point."

Floyd sighed. "This was a mistake," he said morosely.

"You can say that again," Adams agreed. "You ready to go home?"

"No." Floyd shook his head. "We got this far. We should finish the job."

"You need a better cover story," Adams told him. "He didn't buy the coalition thing."

"Buy..." Floyd stared in disbelief. "You don't believe me?"

"I make it a point to never believe you."

"But I'm right," Floyd protested. "They were leaving England and coming here."

"According to you."

"I'm right," Floyd said in irritation.

"You're lying."

Floyd sighed. "Roger was lying," he countered.

"Yeah, I could tell that," Adams said. "The question is, what was he lying about?"

"You're asking my opinion?"

"This is your show."

"Everything," Floyd said. "He was lying about absolutely everything."

DOUBLE-CROSSED

It had been a very long day.

Even Adams was beginning to lose his perpetually calm presence. He was getting more and more irritable towards Floyd, who by contrast was becoming too exhausted to even keep up irritability.

"I don't think I have mentioned that part," Floyd explained. "Smaller planet, lighter gravity, faster spin, shorter days, more stars... and significantly cooler."

"That's the part you have the hardest time dealing with, isn't it," Adams said grimly. "Heat."

"And sunlight," Floyd agreed.

"Did you have a sun?"

"It was a bright shining star in the sky, the crown jewel among thousands of diamonds."

"That's very pretty."

"Thank you."

"So that's why you came to England?"

Floyd smiled wanly. "I liked it there. It's... nice."

"It's not home?"

"Nothing is home."

"I can't imagine having to leave earth like that," Adams mused.

"Neither could I," Floyd said quietly. "Until it happened to me."

"I'm sorry," Adams said.

"It's not your fault," Floyd said swiftly.

"I know that," Adams said, irritated. "But I'm sorry. That you had to go through that, I mean. It must have been rough."

Floyd glanced at the sky. "It still is."

"Oh yes," Adams agreed. "I know that part from experience."

"Sorry," Floyd said shortly.

"Don't worry about it," Adams brushed him off. "If it bothered me that much, I'd arrest you."

"Sure, that's a consolation," Floyd muttered.

"Do you have a plan for what to do next?" Adams asked.

"I never have a plan."

"Unfortunately, I know that, too."

Floyd leaned back and closed his eyes. "I'll think of something," he promised.

"You're not going to sleep, are you?"

"I can think in my sleep."

"No, Floyd," Adams said, standing and pulling him to his feet. "Think of something. Now."

"Um," Floyd squinted into the distance. "Here it comes right now."

"What are you talking about?"

A familiar battered pickup truck bounced to a stop beside them, and Riley poked his head out the window and smiled.

"Having fun?" he asked cheerfully.

"No one will talk to me," Floyd complained. "I don't think they like us."

Riley glanced at Adams, and then at the setting sun.

"Have you got any place to stay tonight?" he asked.

"No," Adams said. "Like he said, they don't like us."

"How about you come back with me?" Riley offered. "I've got plenty of room up at the ranch, and we can talk in peace."

Floyd looked anxiously at Adams. The policeman barely hesitated.

"We'd be much obliged," he said. "It's been a long day."

"I've got another stop or two to make before we got back," Riley said as they climbed into his truck, "but we'll be home in no time."

....

It was two hours later when they finally pulled up in front of a sprawling white house. The yard was dirt but it was surrounded by a wood fence to keep animals out. It was almost completely dark and Floyd had fallen asleep, his head on Adams shoulder. Riley kept grinning at the sight. Adams' endured it patiently.

When he shook Floyd, the alien didn't wake up, and eventually he gave up and half carried him into the house. The ranch house was as large and sprawling on the inside as it looked from the outside, with kitchen, dining room, and living room all melded into one open space. Riley pointed to a couch and Adams put Floyd down. He didn't stir.

81

"Is he all right?" Riley asked, setting down his own burden and coming over.

"I don't know," Adams said, staring down at his companion. "He hasn't been feeling well all day."

Riley put a rough hand on Floyd's forehead and frowned. "He's running a fever," he said. "We'd best let him rest."

....

Floyd woke to the unusual sound of voices murmuring in pleasant conversation above him. He opened his eyes and blinked to see Adams sitting comfortably in an arm chair with a glass of something cold and frothy in his hand, talking to Riley who leaned back in a hardback chair with his feet on the table, smoking.

He was shaking violently, and was freezing cold and very grateful for the blanket someone had placed over him. Neither of the other men had noticed he was awake yet, so he grit his teeth, tried to get his nerves under control, and listened to what they were saying.

"We've had a bit of a rodent problem lately," Riley said, between puffs on his cigarette. "Nothing too serious, of course, but just enough to keep everyone on edge. Never can tell what will follow those sorts."

"Rodents?" Adams asked curiously.

"Mechanical creatures. Sort of like rat-sized cockroaches. No one knows how they work. No one has even managed to capture one. They make a rattling scurrying noise when they move. It terrifies the children."

"What do they do?"

"They cause mischief. They chew things up or carry things away. They're drawn to wiring specifically. They can climb walls, so height is no safety. They're destructive for the sake of destruction."

"Where do they come from?"

"No one knows. Some of the lads tried to follow them, but... that didn't end well."

"What happened?"

"They turned on them and attacked them. One died, and little Peter was blinded."

Adams whistled. "That sounds bad."

"You get used to it after a while. You don't go out after dark, you find ways to encase delicate materials, and you manage. It makes everyone a mite bit protective though, so you understand why they weren't as welcoming as you'd hoped."

"Maybe the rodents are left over from a supervillain occupation earlier?" Adams suggested.

"No," Floyd said abruptly. "It's not chaotic enough for that. This is an ongoing project on the part of a supervillain mastermind."

"You're awake," Adams said.

"Yes," Floyd agreed. "And I'd rather remain that way in the future."

"Are you feeling all right?" Riley asked. "You looked a bit poorly."

"I want to go home," Floyd stated, as though that was the answer to every question.

"Do you want to go back to England?" Adams asked, unsure which home he was referring to.

"No," Floyd snapped. "I'm going to finish this."

"He's helping a friend," Riley reprimanded gently. "And he doesn't look like the type to back down."

"Thank you," Floyd said, smiling. "I'll manage. I always do... somehow."

"Can I get you anything?" Riley asked. "Would you like something to drink?"

"Yes, please," Floyd said eagerly. "Water would be nice."

"Now then," he said, gratefully accepting a glass from his host. "You were discussing mechanical robots?"

Adams glanced at Riley. "How long had you been listening?" he asked.

Floyd shrugged. "No idea. But I know what it means. You have an active mastermind in the area. That's not overly surprising, although I thought all of villains had vacated this area, and it means that Roger was lying through his teeth, but the real question is... why mechanical robots? Why is he staying in hiding? Why isn't there more evidence of supervillain activity? What is he hoping to gain?"

Riley looked at him blankly. "I have no idea what you're talking about, young man," he said slowly.

"That's okay," Floyd said quickly. "I'm just talking."

"He does that sometimes," Adams said. "Hopefully something useful comes out of it."

"It bothers me that Roger would lie," Floyd continued, ignoring them. "I know he's hiding something, I just don't know what. And I don't like it. But it bothers me more that a mastermind would hide. Masterminds are not the hiding type. They at least send out henchmen to intimidate the populace. And why is a mastermind hanging out in this area, anyway? Most decent villains of that scale migrate to the big cities. He must be hiding. But why? Since when do villains hide?"

"How do you know all this?" Riley asked abruptly.

"I don't know anything," Floyd said crossly. "I'm speculating."

"Floyd," Adams said warningly.

"I'm sorry," Floyd apologized."I'm just tired..."

Adams frowned. "Are you sure you can manage this?" he asked.

Floyd glared, and Adams backed down.

There was a crash from the front of the house.

"I'll be right back," Riley said, hauling himself to his feet. "Sounds like there's a critter loose out there."

"If it's one of those robotic mice," Floyd said, laying back down, "Let me look at it."

It wasn't robot mice.

It was a dozen men in dark clothes and ski masks.

Adams thought they looked just like the bus hijackers before someone hit him in the head and he lost consciousness.

....

Joseph S. Adams was not accustomed to waking up with his head pounding to discover himself duct taped to a wooden chair, in the dark.

He was, however, used to listening to Floyd swear, so it took a moment to realize the implications of it.

85

"English, Floyd," he said patiently, once he figured it out.

"They took me by surprise," Floyd said in frustration. "They shouldn't have been able to do that. I took out two of them, and then they pinned me down. I've fought off a dozen supervillains at once and I couldn't handle a couple of henchmen..."

"Relax, Floyd," Adams said. "You weren't at your best."

Floyd swore again.

"Say something useful or be quiet," Adams snapped at him.

"Who are they?" Floyd blurted out.

"I have no idea," Adams said. "They knocked me out. I don't even know where we are."

Floyd sighed and lapsed into silence.

"I prefer something useful," Adams suggested after a minute.

"I'm thinking," Floyd snapped.

"That's an acceptable compromise," Adams relented.

"What happened back there?" Riley asked in the dark. "Who were those guys?"

"They hijacked our bus," Adams explained. "That's why we were walking when you picked us up."

"Do they want something from you?"

"They must, or they wouldn't have broken into your place," Floyd said.

"I'm sorry this happened," Adams said. "I had no idea we'd cause you this much trouble."

"Don't worry about me," Riley chuckled. "I like a little action and adventure every now and then."

"Looks like we're going to get plenty of that," Floyd mused.

"How are you feeling?" Adams asked.

"Show me a supervillain and I'll show you how I'm feeling," Floyd said bitterly.

"You might get that chance," Adams said. "Just don't let me down."

"Sure thing," Floyd promised.

The door opened, and a shaft of light lit up the dark room. Riley was sitting on the floor in front of a bunch of wooden crates, with his hands tied in front of him. Floyd was crouched behind the door, clearly having broken out of his restraints sometime before Adams woke up.

One of the figures in the doorway flipped on a light switch and Adams could see them easily.

"Roger," he said with a sigh.

"What?" Floyd exclaimed, giving away his hiding place. He walked into the open to regard the newcomers himself.

"I don't suppose you're here to rescue us," he said with a sigh.

"You need to catch up with the real world," Roger sneered.

"Yesterday it was all admiration and today you're kidnapping me and stuffing me and my friends into a basement somewhere?" Floyd said incredulously. "I can't believe you, Roger. I thought you had real potential."

"Keep trying to figure me out, wise guy," Roger suggested.

"Oh, I've already figured you out," Floyd said bitterly. "Wannabe henchmen. You're working for the supervillains out of some sense of accomplishment or power, or I don't know. It's sickening."

87

"You done?" Roger asked belligerently.

"He's never done," Adams said.

"Shut your mouth, Brit," one of Roger's companions said. "We're done talking here."

"No, we're not," Floyd said.

"I decide what we're doing or not doing," Roger said pompously.

Floyd raised his eyebrows in disbelief.

"Not now, Floyd," Adams said. "What do you want?" he addressed Roger.

"We've just got a little job that needs doing," Roger said. "I just wanted you to know that when it's over you're free to go."

"Why lock us up in the first place?" Riley asked plaintively. "We were just minding our own business."

"He wasn't," Roger said, pointing at Floyd. "He's putting his nose in where it doesn't belong."

"That," Floyd said crisply, "is the sum of my existence."

"Behave," Roger's unnamed companion said warningly, "and no one will have to get hurt."

"Oh yes?" Floyd snapped. "What if I disagree?"

Roger sighed impatiently. "Obviously, I overdid it yesterday morning when I said I liked your website," he said. "Now you think you're somebody, don't you?"

"Wait, Floyd," Adams said. Floyd shut his mouth without saying anything.

"What sort of project are you worried about us messing up?" Adams asked, addressing Roger.

Roger grinned. "I'm not at leave to disclose that," he said haughtily.

"Floyd," Adams said, attracting his friend's attention. Floyd walked over next to him so they could converse in private.

"They're extortionists," Adams said. "They pretend there's a supervillain and then wring the townspeople for 'protection money.' That's what the other passengers on our bus meant about vigilantes and why they seemed so distrustful. They thought the entire heist was a setup."

Floyd nodded. "Now?" he asked.

"Have at 'em," Adams said.

Floyd turned back around to face Rogers and rubbed his hands gleefully.

"Do you have any more friends waiting on the other side of that door?"

Roger looked puzzled. "No, why?"

"No reinforcements?" Floyd said in mock surprise. "Isn't that a bit risky?"

"Why should it be?"

Floyd spread his hands wide. "Has no one thought to wonder why, while my friends are both bound and incapacitated, I am walking back and forth free to do as I please?"

"He's right!" Roger's friend shouted. "How did he get free?"

That was as far as he got before Floyd came at him, knocking him backwards into the pile of wooden crates. Roger started to retaliate but Floyd tripped him. They tussled on the ground for a brief moment, but Floyd already had the upper hand, and Roger stopped struggling soon enough.

"Floyd," Adams said, distracting him. "Do you mind?"

Floyd switched his attention quickly to untying his friends. From under the crates

Roger's friend cursed heatedly. Floyd dug him out and slammed him against the wall.

"Here's a word of warning for your friend when he wakes up," he hissed. "*Never* underestimate me again. Got it?"

The youth nodded, his eyes wide. Floyd dropped him and waved to Adams and Riley.

"Come on," he said. "We need to get going before the sun rises."

"Why?" Riley asked.

"Because," Floyd said. "I hate sunrises."

Riley glanced inquisitively at Adams, but the latter only shrugged and followed Floyd out.

"It's not a basement," Adams felt compelled to state. "It's a barn."

"I've never been in a barn before," Floyd said dismissively. "I wouldn't know the difference."

Adams decided not to waste energy pursuing the subject. "Where are you going?".

"We have to find the lair of the mastermind," Floyd said. "I need his equipment."

"Floyd," Adams sighed. "I told you. There are no supervillains."

"I know," Floyd said. "But Roger said the same thing. And he's still lying."

He glanced around at the grey, flat expanse. "Something's not right," he murmured. "I just don't know what it is..."

METHOD AND MADNESS

8

"What are we doing back here?" Adams asked, surveying the ruins of the courthouse, surrounded by all kinds of signs prohibiting trespassing and stepping beyond certain boundaries and prophesying death and doom for anyone considering going inside.

Floyd stepped over the carefully erected railing and completely ignored all the signs.

"Looking," he said shortly.

Adams sighed. "Thanks for the ride," he said to Riley. "And I really am sorry about the whole kidnapping thing."

"That's okay," the rugged farmer said with a grin. "I intend to see this thing through. That kid really knows his stuff."

"Come on!" Floyd shouted from inside the rubble. "I found it!"

Adams sighed, and overcame his aversion to going into forbidden places.

"What did you find?" he asked, cautiously stepping through the crumbled wall and wondering if he would ever make it out again.

"Stairs," Floyd said gleefully. "Look around, Joseph. All this has been cleaned out recently."

"The boy is right," Riley said right behind them. "I saw this place before they put up all those fancy guardrails and it looked like nuclear war in here."

"Anyone got a torch?" Floyd asked.

No one did.

"There's one back in the truck," Riley offered.

"He won't wait for you," Adams said. "Better just make do with what we've got."

Floyd started down the stairs into the unknown and the dark. Adams followed along behind, keeping one hand on the wall. He could hear Riley behind him, breathing heavily.

Floyd vanished into the darkness ahead of him, but Adams kept steadily on, checking each step before he put his weight on it. Finally he reached the bottom, and turned to make sure Riley made it down safely as well. The room suddenly flooded with light, and he looked over his shoulder to see Floyd grinning like a kid with a new bike.

"Told you!" he said excitedly. "It's all here. This is where he was hiding."

"Roger?" Adams asked, dreading the answer.

"The mastermind!" Floyd corrected. "Roger didn't make all this."

The walls were lined with monitors showing different parts of the town. Computers were lined up under a desk, linked together. In a cage in the corner were dozens of dormant robotic rodents.

Floyd sat in front of the monitors, delighted with his find.

"What are you looking for?" Adams asked.

"The coalition," Floyd said.

"No," Adams repeated himself. "What are you really looking for?"

"The coalition," Floyd said stubbornly.

"I told you, you need a new cover story."

"It's not a cover."

"I know when you're lying."

"I'm not lying."

"I wish you would tell me the truth Floyd. I've done enough for you this week."

"There's a coalition out there," Floyd said, searching through the records. "And I'm going to find it."

"You think it's here?"

"I do."

"What do you think they're up to?"

Floyd grinned. "Why don't we go ask them?"

Adams sighed and pulled up a crate to sit on. Riley had already made himself comfortable and was smoking a cigarette.

"What are you looking for?" Adams asked Floyd.

"Suspicious activity," Floyd answered absently, tweaking the controls on the monitor.

"Define suspicious."

"You're the cop," Floyd said. "You tell me."

Riley chuckled. "I didn't know you were an officer of the law," he said. "I'd have hid my contraband before I invited you into my house."

"London Met," Adams sighed. "I'm out of my jurisdiction here."

"Oh, okay," Riley said. "That's a relief."

"I could report you to the local police though," Adams warned.

"Nah," Floyd interjected. "That wouldn't do any good. They're bought off."

"How do you know that?" Adams asked.

Floyd shrugged. "Call it a hunch."

"Who's bought them off?"

"Either the supervillains or your extortionists. But it's entirely possible that Roger and his buddies are also paid by the supervillains."

"Why would they do that?"

"Who?"

"Why would the supervillains hire some local gang?"

"To attract attention away from them," Floyd said. "So that people would think exactly what you thought and not dig any deeper."

"Clever," Adams said, rolling his eyes.

"Yes," Floyd agreed. "Very clever. And effective. I almost fell for it myself."

"Did you really?"

"I said almost." Floyd glared. "And in my defense, I was not feeling well."

"Are you feeling better now?"

"For the time being, yes. But let's get this over with as soon as possible, shall we?"

"Are you making any progress?" Adams asked restlessly.

"Mmm," Floyd said noncommittally.

"I can see you gave a lot of thought to that reply."

Riley chuckled again. "Let the boy work," he said. "He knows what he's doing."

Floyd paused to give Riley an appreciative glance. "Thank you for that," he said. "Very few people appreciate what I do."

"Anytime, kid," Riley said amiably.

"But stop calling me kid," Floyd said. "I'm not that young."

"How old are you?"

"I don't know," Floyd muttered, turning back to the monitors.

"Then how do you know you're not a kid?"

Floyd made no response.

"Not answering that one, eh?"

"There," Floyd said, pointing at something on the computer screen.

"What?" Adams got up and looked.

"I know him," Floyd said triumphantly. "He left London the day before we did. And he's here. That should be all the evidence you need, Joseph."

"It's not," Adams said.

"Wet blanket," Floyd accused. "But I also have an address. I hacked into his email account..."

"Who's?"

"The mastermind's. He calls himself Super Villain, by the way. Cliche if there ever was one."

"Wait," Adams said, holding up his hands. "Supervillains have emails?"

Floyd turned to look at him. "This is the twenty-first century," he said patiently. "*Everyone* has email."

"What in the world does a supervillain use an email address for?"

"Joseph," Floyd said. "What does anyone use an email address for?"

"But—" Adams protested.

Floyd sighed. "I don't have time for this."

"Okay, fine," Adams said. "What does this particular email say?"

"It's a meeting time and place," Floyd said, scribbling rapidly.

"And we're going there?" Adams asked in resignation.

"Oh, yes." Floyd's smile lit up his eyes, and in the depths of that smile Adams could see trouble of all kinds along with inescapable impending disaster. "Let's go!"

He dashed towards the stairs.

"Floyd!" Adams shouted. The alien paused and looked back, that disastrous grin still spread across his face like icing from a cupcake at a two-year-old's birthday party.

Adams shook his head to get that image out of his mind.

"What?" Floyd said impatiently.

"Don't you think you're being a bit reckless?" Adams asked.

"Reckless is my middle name," Floyd said carelessly.

"No, it's Lewis," Adams corrected. "Reckless is what gets you killed."

"I don't understand what you're going on about."

"If there really is a supervillain coalition don't you think you should come up with a better plan than dashing into their meeting?" Adams pointed out. "That sounds like a good way to get killed."

"You should listen to him, sonny," Riley said, putting out his cigarette and standing up. "If you just go rushing in there you're liable to do something stupid."

"That's what I do," Floyd said, his good mood unabated. "I do something stupid. That's how I take out the bad guys."

"Floyd," Adams said warningly.

"Come on!" Floyd repeated, and finished his dash up the stairs. Sighing, Adams followed, Riley close behind.

Riley got in the driver's side of the truck, Floyd slid into the middle beside him, and Adams got the passenger side as usual.

"Where are we going?" Riley asked, starting the engine. Floyd passed him the address he'd written down. Riley glanced at it. "The old Crowley place, eh?" he said inquisitively. "No one's been out there in years. The owner was killed, you know," he offered, keeping his eyes on the road. "Back when all this started."

Floyd sobered up instantly. "I'm sorry," he said quietly.

"I didn't know him real well," Riley said. "He wasn't a personal friend."

Floyd nodded absently.

"But it's something you should keep in mind, young man," he continued. Floyd glanced at him sharply. "It's not all fun and games," Riley explained. "These villains are dangerous, and people usually get killed when they're around."

"I know," Floyd said quietly.

"Just don't forget it," Riley cautioned.

"I never do," Floyd said tightly.

Riley nodded to himself. "You're a good kid," he said. "I hope you have a very happy life when all this is over."

"I hope I don't have to wait that long," Floyd said, his grin returning.

"You got a girlfriend?" Riley asked.

Floyd shook his head.

"Do you do this kind of thing often?"

"Yes," Adams answered for him.

"Just as well then," Riley said. "A girl would be a liability to you, if they ever decided to target you."

"I know," Floyd said softly. "I know."

"Best just wait," Riley repeated. "It can't go on forever."

"Five years," Floyd said bitterly.

"Eh?"

"That's how long," Floyd explained. "Five years is the longest it can be sustained, but no one knows why..."

"You're out of my area of expertise, young man," Riley said laughing. "Just take my word for it and be cautious about involving anyone else in these harum scarum games of yours.

"Well, here we are."

Riley pulled up in front of a sprawling ranch similar to his own, only more decrepit.

"Not the house," Floyd said. "Too obvious."

He pointed further down the road. "We'll try that first."

Riley parked in front of the barn as instructed.

"Come on," Floyd said impatiently, and Adams opened the door and let him out.

"Don't you think we should try to figure out what we're doing before we—"

Floyd bolted towards the barn.

"—go rushing in there?" Adams finished, rolling his eyes.

"Floyd!" Riley shouted, cupping his hands round his mouth. Floyd came to a dead stop and looked back over his shoulder. Adams beckoned him back.

"What?" Floyd asked, trotting over. "Let's go."

"*If* there is a coalition," Adams said carefully, "Don't you think you should have a better plan than to just go barreling in like you own the place?"

"What's wrong with that plan?" Floyd shrugged. "I'm sure I can handle it."

"If that's a supervillain coalition," Adams repeated. "It's a pretty dangerous force, isn't it?"

"Nah," Floyd said dismissively. "They might not even be here."

"I still think—" Adams suggested, but Floyd was already walking away, so he gave up and followed at a cautious distance.

Floyd pulled open the huge barn doors slightly and disappeared inside. Adams hesitated, but eventually decided that waiting outside wasn't a viable option and followed him in. He froze just inside the door.

"Uh oh," Floyd said.

"NOT WHAT I EXPECTED"

Dark eyes peered down from the loft. Hideous creatures snaked their way through the hay that carpeted the barn floor. Figures that could barely be recognized as human draped their contorted limbs over the beams that stretched across the open space. Men and women in business suits and evening gowns sat around a rickety table at the far end of the barn from Floyd. Something fluttered around the bare light bulb that hung over the table.

Floyd stood just inside the door, petrified by what he saw. Adams stood next to him, glancing around nervously. Riley stood behind them, unsure how to react.

"Uh oh," Floyd said.

"You already mentioned that," Adams hissed.

"I wasn't expecting this," Floyd confessed.

"You've been looking for a supervillain coalition," Adams said. "What were you expecting?"

Floyd shrugged and didn't answer.

"No," Adams said, realization sinking in. "Oh no you don't. It really was a cover story all along!"

"Joseph," Floyd said feebly.

"No," Adams repeated. "I can't believe this. What *were* you really after, Floyd?"

"You didn't believe in it either!" Floyd argued.

"So?" Adams said. "It's my job to not believe in the things you are convinced are true. Of course I didn't believe in it. That's to be expected. The question is, what were *you* expecting to find here?"

Floyd tried to answer and came up empty handed. One of the supervillains detached himself from the group and came over, leering. The rest continued to ignore their presence.

"I don't believe this," Adams repeated. "Who is that guy, Floyd?"

"You," Floyd said, ignoring his friend and striding forward to meet Two-Face. "We end this. Now."

"Really?" Two-Face grinned. "Now?"

"You're going to start by giving back what you stole."

"Oh, that," Two-Face laughed. "Now you're willing to fight me equally, now that I've sufficiently irritated you?"

"Floyd," Adams said insistently. "Look at me."

Reluctantly Floyd glanced back at him.

"I told you to stay out of it," Adams said sternly.

"Yeah, and I didn't listen to you," Floyd said in frustration. "You should be used to that by now."

Adams face darkened with anger, but he was spared any further reprimand by Two-Face, who took advantage of Floyd's distraction to jerk him around and hit him in the face. Floyd stumbled backwards and landed flat on his back in the hay.

"Let's do this," Two-Face said, showing his snarling face. "Now."

Floyd started to get up, and Two-Face kicked him the chest.

Floyd bit back a cry of pain and stopped moving.

"Floyd?" Adams asked uncertainly.

Two-Face switched back to his laughing face and dragged Floyd over to one of the posts that held the barn up. Skeins of thin twine were hung over one of the beams and he used it to tie Floyd's hands behind the post. Laughing again at Adams and Riley, he strolled back to the other side of the barn where the rest of the supervillains were studiously ignoring them.

"Floyd," Adams said anxiously, kneeling in front of his friend. "Floyd, answer me."

"I'm okay," Floyd said, smiling slightly. "I just wanted him to stop hitting me."

"So now you're tied up?" Adams said incredulously.

Floyd shrugged. "You can untie me," he said carelessly.

"Yes, I can," Adams said. "And that makes no sense. Why doesn't anyone care why we're here?"

"I don't know," Floyd said thoughtfully.

He regarded them for a moment and then shifted restlessly. "Untie me?" he asked pleadingly.

"No," Adams said decisively, sitting down cross-legged.

"No?" Floyd repeated in disbelief.

"No," Adams said firmly. "Not until you explain what is going on here."

Floyd sighed. "I don't know."

"Figure it out then."

Floyd looked around, squinting up into the loft, and carefully regarding the squirmy things in the hay.

"I don't know," he said again.

"Floyd," Adams said warningly.

"Let me think," Floyd said impatiently. "And be quiet."

Riley sat on an overturned bucket and lit a cigarette.

An overweight supervillain in an expensive suit stood up an addressed the assembly.

"What on earth—" Adams started.

Floyd shushed him.

"I have found," he said laboriously, "That the secret to conveying a properly evil presence is all about knowing in advance what you intend to say, and projecting your words with meaning and intent.

"In my experience, too many supervillains ignore the importance of a well prepared speech. They appear on the scene of their crime without knowing exactly what they're going to say, and stammer their way through the scenario looking like amateurs. The villain who knows exactly what to say is a villain that is truly fearful."

He finished his speech with a little bow and sat back down to the sound of appreciative applause, and a few noises that might have been applause if the creatures making them had possessed the proper appendages.

"That's just creepy," Adams whispered to Floyd.

"No, it makes a lot of sense," Floyd whispered back. "He's completely right. Especially when I'm around, an ill-prepared speech can ruin an otherwise perfectly evil occasion."

"You're creepy," Adams amended.

"Hush," Floyd said. "Someone else is talking."

"We should get out of here," Adams muttered.

"Hush," Floyd reprimanded.

"Villains, supervillains, henchmen, and creatures," a new villain said, standing and bowing. He wore a red coat, black gloves, and had goggles pushed up on his forehead. "So many villains overlook the evil laugh. That's about standards, you know? Like Mr. Heavyset said here, being a supervillain is more than just blowing things up and making a lot of people miserable. It's about presenting yourself as a professional, and it takes work. If your laugh sounds like a girl on her first date, then you obviously don't have what it takes to be a real villain."

He sat down smugly, and the villains applauded again.

"I don't believe this," Adams hissed. "I'm sitting in the middle of a support group for evil tactics."

"That's it!" Floyd shouted.

The assembly shushed him in unison.

"That's it," Floyd whispered. "It's not a coalition at all. It's a support group. That's why they're ignoring us; they're embarrassed that we caught them at home so to speak, and they're hoping that if they pretend we don't exist we'll just go away and never come back."

"I suggest we do just that then," Adams said, working on the ropes keeping Floyd tied up.

"No," Floyd said. "I've got to get your papers back from Two-Face."

"It's none of your concern, Floyd," Adams said tightly. "I can't believe you dragged me all the way over here for that."

"Fine," Floyd said, glaring at him. "*You* get your papers back from Two-Face. They're your responsibility, after all."

Adams broke away from his gaze and went back to the knots.

The next villain to stand up was mostly snake. He balanced on his tail, with two short legs sticking out in front of him.

"Being properly evvvvvil," he hissed, "is also about appearance. You cannot make the right impressssssssion in blue jeanssss and a t-ssssssshirt. Gaudy cosssssstumessss alssso make the wrong impressssion. Any good villain mussst be aware of the fear and ressssspect he wisssshes to command. People mussst recognize that we are a force to be reckoned with the moment we walk into the room, and before we even commenccce the evil laugh, or our eviiiil speechesssss."

"Now that's complete garbage," Floyd said dismissively. "Bearing is a factor, yes, but everyone knows that appearance has nothing to do with it. I don't dress like a fashion model and I'm a force to be reckoned with."

"You're hardly a standard for good villains," Adams added, finally finishing with the twine. Floyd rubbed his wrists and stared ruefully at the deep lines in his arms.

"You're no expert," he retorted.

"Are you seriously going to sit here and critique them?" Adams asked.

"Don't make fun," Floyd said, offended. "Some of this is really quite good. I should put it on my blog."

"Please tell me we're not going to spend the whole day here," Adams begged.

"No," Floyd said quickly, scrambling to his feet. "I'm going after Two-Face."

He started off, and then automatically hesitated, waiting. Adams didn't say anything.

Floyd turned around. "No parting jabs?" he said, spreading his hands. "No remarks about how pointless it is and how it's your life and I should just get out of here while I can?"

Adams shook his head. "Go get them," he said, smiling.

"Thank you," Floyd said graciously. "I will."

"Excuse me," he said, sauntering over to the table. Hundreds of eyes turned to look at him.

"You are not on the agenda," a woman in a red evening gown said strictly. "If you wish to make a speech we can put you down for next time."

"Oh no," Floyd laughed. "You misunderstand me. I'm not coming next time. I'm just here to crash your party."

His announcement was met with cold hostility.

"What?" he spread his hands. "No reaction to that."

"Please sit down and stop being disruptive," the red-gowned woman said sternly.

"Okay," Floyd stuck his hands in his pockets. "Fine. Be that way. Can't say much for your hospitality."

He sauntered back towards Adams, passing Two-Face as he did so. The villain wasn't expecting him to do anything, and was carefully maintaining a look of cold hostility which matched that in the eyes of every other villain in the place. By the time he realized he should be paying attention, it was too late, Floyd had the upper hand, and the fight was just about over.

Floyd found the papers inside the villain's shirt, and gave him an extra kick for good measure. He scurried back to Riley and Adams and handed the policeman the papers.

"That's what you're in trouble over, yeah?" he said breathlessly.

Adams skimmed them briefly. "Yeah," he confirmed. "They're all here. Thanks, Floyd…"

"You know what?" Floyd said. "Skip the thanks. I have a better idea."

"What's that?" Adams asked curiously.

Floyd glanced at Two-Face, who had regained his feet and was snarling, and then looked back at Adams.

"Let's get out of here," he said anxiously. "As quickly as possible, if you please."

'1HOME AGAIN, 1HOME AGAIN, JIGGEDY-JOG"

"Are they following us?" Floyd asked for the fifteenth time.

"No Floyd," Adams said patiently. "No one is following us."

Floyd glanced behind them anxiously. "You're sure?"

"I'm sure."

He ran his fingers through his hair. "I don't see why they would let us get away so easily," he said distractedly. "We interrupted them, discovered them, humiliated them..."

"And they'd rather forget all about us," Adams said soothingly. "Now relax."

"I can't relax. I'm too tense to relax. You're sure no one's following us?"

"If you ask that again," Adams said gently, "I will smack you."

Floyd sighed. "What about Rogers and his gang?" he said. "What are they up to?"

109

"I don't know, Floyd."

"Is he all right?" Riley asked.

"I think the heat's getting to him again," Adams said wearily. "I'll be very glad to get him home."

"You're going back to England then?"

Adams nodded. "We got what we came for."

"And all those things in the barn back there, what about them?"

Adams shrugged. "They're not hurting you," he said. "I imagine that when their little retreat is over they'll go back to their own parts of the world with new resolve to do evil deeds with style and flair."

"Roger has to be stopped," Floyd said. "Can't have ordinary people playing at being villains. Too dangerous. Scares people..."

Riley chuckled. "Don't worry about that, young man," he said. "We'll take care of those young whippersnappers. Never you fear."

"What are you going to do?" Floyd asked.

"You may be an expert when it comes to supervillains, but I know a thing or two about handling ordinary ruffians," Riley said ambiguously. "You leave them to me."

"And the robotic robots?"

"I'm sure Roger knows how to deal with them."

"Maybe I should go back," Floyd said, "and disable them for you. They can be nasty, vicious creatures if you don't understand—"

"It's okay," Riley said, putting a hand on his shoulder. "If I have any problems, I'll email you."

"How will you know how to get in touch with me?"

"You have a website, kid."

"Oh yeah, right.

"Wait a minute," Floyd straightened up, lucid for a moment. "*You* read my blog?"

Riley laughed. "No, I don't," he said. "But I will. I think what you're doing is a fine thing. More people need to know how to take care of themselves instead of depending on protection from thugs and governments."

"The man makes a good point," Floyd said, leaning back and closing his eyes. "Are we going home?"

"Yes," Adams said. "We're going home."

"Back to London?"

"Yes."

"You're sure there's no one following us?"

EPILOGUE

"You're late," Adams said, without setting down his newspaper.

"You know what?" Floyd said in irritation. "I'm not late. Because I'm not even here yet. I'm not here, because you can't see me, because you haven't even looked over that paper of yours. Is that my paper?"

"Yes," Adams said. "I like to keep up with your actions, you know, even the pointlessly trivial ones."

He tossed the newspaper aside. "How are you doing?"

"That's a subjective question," Floyd said evasively.

Adams didn't repeat the question.

"Better," Floyd blurted out, unable to hold up under the steady stare of the police officer. "It's good to be back."

"Good," Adams said. "Got into any trouble lately?"

"No, it's been pretty quiet. Not everyone is back from the support group, I suppose. How about you? Back in uniform, I see."

"My suspension was revoked when I produced the missing papers."

"Did you tell them how you retrieved them?"

"No," Adams said crisply. "I did not."

Floyd shrugged. "Have it your own way."

"I suppose I owe you an apology," Adams said slowly.

Floyd looked alarmed.

"If it hadn't been for you things might have turned out," he hesitated, "much worse. I didn't make it easy for you to help me and... you did it anyway. I owe you for that."

Floyd remained uncomfortably silent.

"And I've been thinking about what you said," Adams continued. "About friends..."

Floyd laughed suddenly. Adams looked up in confusion.

"I don't believe it," Floyd said in explanation. "I've got a friend on the police force."

"I wouldn't put it that way," Adams said warningly. "I've still got my eye on you."

"I don't mind," Floyd said, uncharacteristically serious. He held out his hand across the table. "Just don't expect me to leave the country on your behalf again."

Adams shook his head solemnly. "Agreed," he said.

They were interrupted by the sound of the door slamming, a crash, and the scream of a waitress.

"Floyd!" A heavy hand clamped down on Floyd shoulder and threw him against the neighboring table. Two-Face half scowled, half sneered into Floyd's face.

"We have some unfinished business."

ƧNEAꝀ ᴘEEꝀ

Don't miss
Supervillain of the Day: Book 5
"Dreams and Shadows"
Coming September 5th, 2013!

Floyd woke up with his skin on fire, his head exploding, and the unsettling feeling that the world had ended without him. He tried to sit up, and decided that was a bad idea, opting to lay still for the moment instead. He opened and closed his eyes several times, wondering why it made no difference in the darkness surrounding him.

The darkness was unsettling. It was thick, and heavy, like a stage curtain or a funeral shroud. He breathed it into his lungs and it choked him, seeping into—

He jerked away from the nightmare, and the sudden movement made his head throb. The unsettling feeling grew into a sort of panic; something was very, very wrong here.

But the thought drained away quietly, like water emptying out of a cracked vase. It went and left him drained, still, waiting like smooth sand for the next wave to crash.

When it came he sat up suddenly, gasping for breath, nearly crying out with the fear of it. His panic drove him to his feet in spite of the sudden vertigo that hit him, and he ran headlong into a wall he couldn't see, clawing for a way out, desperate to escape.

For a brief moment cold rationality hit him like a breath of fresh air, and he knew he was being controlled, that his thoughts and feelings were not his own. But before he could process what exactly that meant the ability to think was stripped away from him, and he sank down against the wall, uncaring.

The third time should have been the most brutal. The unnatural sensation of panic should have reduced Floyd to a cowering puddle of fear in the corner, but the effect had already grown old. He snatched the sensation neatly out of his brain and shoved it into a corner with all the other nasty things he tried to forget about. Out loud he said:

"Stop toying with me. It won't work."

And then suddenly he was alone in his own mind, and in a dark room.

He scrambled to his feet, eager to explore his surroundings, and promptly fell down. He sprawled on the floor, swore at the ceiling, and remembered that his head hurt, his skin was on fire, and it felt like the world had ended without him.

Which probably meant that he'd been killed in some nasty fashion, slept his way back to life, and missed the ending of the world.

That would explain why it was dark, in any case.

Whoever was enjoying messing around in his head decided to try a new tactic. Instead of fear he was suddenly hit with an overwhelming feeling of...

Shame.

He remembered in vivid detail every instance where he had done something stupid, and stood in Adams' office being berated for it. He could remember exactly how it felt wishing he hadn't done it, because in the end the prank wasn't worth the scolding, and—

Floyd laughed aloud. Because he could also remember every time he'd pulled something off and had gotten away with it, and those time had been worth the scoldings for the others.

He could feel the displeasure of his tormentor like a tangible thing in the darkness, and it only fed his self-satisfaction. Standing more carefully this time, and prepared to fight off his physical weaknesses, he finally began to explore his surroundings.

The walls were smooth, and cold, and definitely metallic. So was the floor. Circumventing the room he determined that there was no discernible form of egress. There was probably a sliding panel opening only from the outside.

Completing his inspection he sat down again, and tried to process the information he'd accumulated. He'd been captured. He was in a metal box. Escape from the metal box was impossible. The metal box contained nothing besides himself. There were no sharp edges anywhere. His captor was some kind of telepath.

Quite possibly his prison had been built specifically for him.

He had no memory of the events leading up to his capture.

It was the last bit that bothered him the most. Short-term memory loss was normal, especially after serious injury, but it didn't mean he had to like it. And he'd been awake for some time now—hadn't he? It was impossible to measure time in the box, in the dark, but between the time he'd taken to examine his surroundings and the distractions provided by his mysterious host surely it had been an hour or two.

He cleared his mind for a moment, and waited to see if his captor would make another assault. Nothing happened.

He pondered possible routes of escape. Nothing plausible came to mind.

Floyd got bored very quickly. When he was bored he had a tendency to do things that could be considered stupid.

"Is that all you've got?" he shouted to the unseen entity that had him captive. "I mean, really. You're the first supervillain to successfully capture and imprison me, and that's all you planned to do to me?"

His voice echoed off the metal walls and rung loudly in his ears, and when the echoes faded there was no reply.

"I mean really, it's a bit insulting," he continued rashly. "Where are the threats? The evil laughter? The crowd of snarling henchmen all bowing to your genius? Where are all the demands and instruments of torture?"

The fear was like a howling wind that twisted around him like a tornado, and squeezed until he couldn't breathe, until his blood froze in his veins. It was like every nightmare he'd ever had, relived in vivid, waking detail. It was like every time he'd died, afraid he would never wake up.

Then it was gone, leaving him weak and shaking, and as he pulled himself to his knees he whispered:

"That was stupid."

Hollow laughter rang in his ears. It was impossible to determine where it was coming from. He knew only that it wasn't his own.

Before he had time to collect his thoughts he was jerked away. Away from the prison cell, away from his own body. He was standing in a last desperate stand against the supervillains, and he was watching Joseph Adams die.

To report a supervillain
or learn more about the series,
visit:

supervillainoftheday.com

A NOTE ABOUT ENGLAND

Being an American writing about England is one of the most terrifying and exhilarating things I have ever done. I've done my best to be as accurate as possible when setting this series in London, but we're all human and can make mistakes. If you're an expert or a resident of England and you find an error in this narrative, be sure to let me know about it! I'll take the correction under consideration when writing future novels, and possibly even correct the error in the omnibus version.

Submit errors using the form provided on supervillainoftheday.com and you could earn yourself a copy of the ebook version of the next novel in the series!

ABOUT THE AUTHOR

Katie is a writer of many talents, constantly branching out into new fields and genres. She primarily writes novels and short stories in the science fiction and fantasy genres, along with an assortment of hilarious and sentimental poetry. When she's not writing she's acting, directing, singing, playing her Celtic harp or songwriting, often engaging in more than one at a time. She lives in the beautiful hills of Kentucky with her parents and eight siblings.

Visit her website at katielynndaniels.com

Or follow her on twitter @danielskatie